"What in [...] doing i[...]

"Once we get settled, [...] said to Sam as they approached the small house where Nicki had put them, "we should go across the street, see what we can turn up."

Sam went upstairs, the wood creaking under his lanky frame.

Dean dug the key out of his pants pocket and slid the key into the large sliding door. Pushing it aside, he entered the room, which was a bit stuffy. While it was much warmer than it was at Bobby's, it was cool by Florida standards, so opening the window did the trick. Last time, Dean and Dad had been here in summertime, and the air conditioner was absolutely necessary.

Reaching up, Dean yanked on the chain that started the ceiling fan going, and he left the big sliding door open but closed the screen door to keep the bugs out. He considered warning Sam about the mosquitoes, then decided it would be more fun for him to learn that lesson his own self.

"What in blazes are you doing in my house?"

Whirling around, Dean saw a man wearing a blue cap, a blue jacket, and white pants. Dean also clearly saw the wall behind the man.

In all his years of hunting, Dean had encountered many a spirit. Few of them had ever been this—well, coherent.

"Uh—"

"I asked you a question, young man. This is my abode, and I wish to know what you're doing in it!"

"And you are?"

"Captain Terrence Naylor, of course! Now answer my blasted question!"

SUPERNATURAL Books
From HarperEntertainment

BONE KEY

WITCH'S CANYON

NEVERMORE

THE SUPERNATURAL BOOK OF MONSTERS,
SPIRITS, DEMONS, AND GHOULS

SUPERNATURAL ™
BONE KEY

Keith R.A. DeCandido

Based on the hit CW series SUPERNATURAL
created by Eric Kripke

HARPER

ENTERTAINMENT

An Imprint of HarperCollinsPublishers

This is a work of fiction. Names, characters, places, and incidents are products of the author's imagination or are used fictitiously and are not to be construed as real. Any resemblance to actual events, locales, organizations, or persons, living or dead, is entirely coincidental.

HARPER ⬤ ENTERTAINMENT

An Imprint of HarperCollins*Publishers*
195 Broadway
New York, NY 10007

ISBN 978-0-06-143503-4

HarperCollins®, HARPER ⬤ ENTERTAINMENT™, and Harper-Entertainment™ are trademarks of HarperCollins Publishers.

First HarperEntertainment paperback printing: September 2008

Printed in the United States of America

Visit HarperEntertainment on the World Wide Web at
www.harpercollins.com

10

Dedicated to Michael McCloud—thanks for all the fine entertainment at the Schooner's Wharf and elsewhere during my many trips to Key West.

Acknowledgments

The usual thanks: to my wonderful editors John Morgan, Chris Cerasi, and Emily Krump; to my even more wonderful agent Lucienne Diver; to Eric Kripke, Ben Edlund, John Shiban, the amazing Sera Gamble, and the various other scribes who chronicle the weekly adventures of Sam and Dean Winchester on *Supernatural*; and to Jared Padalecki, Jensen Ackles, and Jim Beaver, for providing face and voice and character for Sam, Dean, and Bobby.

Thanks to the various online *Supernatural* resources, from the official *Supernatural* site at supernatural.warnerbros.com to the "Super-wiki" at supernatural.oscillating.net to the *Supernatural* entries on the main Wikipedia to the various other folks on the Internet who support, discuss, overanalyze, and lust over the show, particularly the folks on the various *Supernatural* communities on LiveJournal and the forums at TV.com, TelevisionWithoutPit.com, and the

Supernatural FaNily Club at spnfanily.yuku.com. Also thanks to the websites for the Hemingway Home and Museum (www.hemingwayhome.com), the Bull and Whistle (www.thebullandwhistle.com), and the Little White House (www.trumanlittlewhitehouse.com) for background on those locales and to the official Ernest Hemingway website (www.ernesthemingway.com). Huge thanks to the good folks at the Key West branch of the Monroe County Public Library, from which I gained much of my knowledge of the lives and times of wreckers and of the Calusa Indians, and to artist Theodore Morris for his visual renditions of the Calusa (which can be seen at www.floridalosttribes. com). And finally, thanks to Rachael, a.k.a. RaeSof-Sunshine, who provided a transcript and breakdown of the show's exorcism ritual on her blog at raesof-sunshine.blogspot.com.

Thanks to my beta readers for invaluable feed-back: Constance Cochran, Kara Cox, Jen Craw-ford, GraceAnne Andreassi DeCandido, Heidi Ellis, Marina Frants, Nicholas Knight (author of the excellent *Supernatural: The Official Companion* for seasons one and two), and Lesley McBain. And thanks to the many and varied folks who e-mailed me after *Nevermore* came out; hope you enjoy the follow-up . . .

Thanks to *Kyoshi* Paul and everyone at the dojo for enlivening my body and my spirit.

And thanks to them that live with me, both human and feline, for everything.

Key West, Florida, is my home
And you know I never ever want to roam
Where the ladies are lovely, and drinking
is my favorite sport
(Well, second favorite . . .)
I'd rather be here
Just drinking a beer
Than be freezing my ass in the north

—Michael McCloud
"The Conch Republic Song"

Historian's Note

This novel takes place a week after the third-season episode *A Very Supernatural Christmas*.

FIRST PROLOGUE

Two hundred years ago . . .

The chief priest sat in the canoe as the boy rowed to the sacred island.

The Calusa had constructed the island themselves, amidst the many natural islands that trailed off the home peninsula. Like their homes and their tools, the island was built from the shells that the water gave them. The water also gave them food and transportation.

Now the sacred island was one of the few refuges left. Once, it had been the place where warriors gathered and where their efforts were planned and blessed by the Three Gods.

There were times that the chief priest wondered if the Three Gods had forsaken them. He did not hold such blasphemy for long. But as he watched the leader, his only son, wither away, covered in the pockmarks that the outsiders had brought to them, it was hard not to at least consider that the Three Gods had forsaken them, that the Calusa were no longer worthy of the gods' gifts.

His son would be dead soon. Even if the outsiders' diseases did not take him, as they had the war chief, then the Creek or the Yamasee would. Once, such lesser tribes feared the mighty Calusa. Then the outsiders came. They, too, feared the Calusa, who rejected their trinkets and their single god.

But the Creek and the Yamasee were weak, so they accepted the outsiders' gifts—including their weapons. The Calusa were once feared in part because of their weapons made with the shells provided by the water, but the metal shells of the outsiders were mightier than the shells of the sea.

Between the raids and the sickness, the Calusa were ravaged. They could no longer protect their friends, such as the Seminoles and the Tequesta, and they could no longer defeat their enemies.

The chief priest knew that soon they would all be dead. Perhaps within two seasons.

So he needed to prepare, as he and the other priests had decided.

"We are here," the boy said. The chief priest looked up, having fallen into a reverie and not realized that they had arrived.

"Come," the chief priest said, slowly rising to his feet on old bones that creaked and cracked.

The boy helped the chief priest steady himself as they disembarked, then he retrieved the large gourds containing the items that the chief priest had requested he bring with him.

When they were on the hard land of the sacred island, the boy said, "Tell me what I must do."

"The shadow soul and the reflection soul are of no use to us," the chief priest said. "They are given to the animals of the land and sea to live new lives. But the eye soul remains, and it is that which we must harness." The chief priest put a hand on the boy's chest. "We give our lives today so that one day the Calusa may have their revenge."

Standing proud, the boy said, "I would rather die in the service of the Calusa than wither away from the outsiders' sickness."

With a smile, the chief priest added, "Or be bloodied by the outsiders' weapons?" Before the boy could protest, the chief priest reassured him. "It does not matter. Your courage is already well-known to us all. It is why the Three Gods chose you. And it is why, when our people are gone, you and I shall remain behind to bind the eye souls of our people together."

Nodding, the boy said, "I am ready."

First, the boy took out the masks. Calusa masks covered the entire face with painted wood, with

holes only for the eyes, to keep that soul unfettered. For the priest, the mask was blue, white, and
red, with an open mouth rendered to symbolize his
conversations with the Three Gods. As for the boy,
his mask was red, black, and white, and portrayed
the fierceness of a warrior born.

The chief priest removed the three daggers from
the gourd, handing one to the boy and holding the
other two in his hands. Then he began the dance
and the chant to the gods. The boy followed along,
mirroring the chief priest's movements.

After they had completed three circles, the chief
priest sliced open his left wrist with the dagger in
his right hand, then reached out and did the same
to the boy's left hand.

At a nod from the chief priest, he and the boy
both then lunged for each other. The dagger in
the priest's right hand plunged into the boy's chest
even as the boy's dagger plunged into the priest's.

The chief priest felt the life blood drain from
him, and he knew that the Three Gods had *not*
forsaken him, for if they had, they would not have
provided him with the means of avenging the
Calusa upon the world.

When the time was right . . .

SECOND PROLOGUE

Six months ago . . .

The demons gathered.

Azazel had told them that it would be happening soon. Not everyone believed Azazel, of course. For all his power, he was still a demon, and demons lied—no one knew that better than the demons themselves. And even if he wasn't lying, not all the hellspawn were convinced that the old bastard would be able to pull it off.

Some thought the plan too convoluted—corrupting a whole bunch of children and having them compete with each other to see who would be most worthy to lead Azazel's army.

Some just didn't like the plan, especially since it called for them being led by a human. Yes, it was a human handpicked (and handcrafted, in many ways) by Azazel, but still a human. Most demons had long since lost whatever connection to humanity they once had, and those who had some dim recollection of their time on the mortal plane before they were sent to hell didn't exactly look back on that time with fondness.

But many believed in Azazel. They were willing to put their faith in him if it meant *getting out*. They were willing to subvert their wills to a human if it meant *getting out*. They would stand here at the edge of the gate, waiting, waiting, *waiting,* as long as it meant *getting the hell out.*

The gate had been put there by a human who was probably the most hated of that species among demonkind: Samuel Colt. A hunter who'd constructed a pistol that could kill demons—not just send them back to hell, which was certainly bad enough, but actually *end* them—and who'd constructed the Devil's Gate that kept the pathway between Earth and hell closed, forcing demons to more subtle means of entering the mortal plane.

Most demons were too lazy, too incompetent, or too stupid to contrive subtle means of escape. Or they simply didn't want to deal with the *agita* of having to follow the exact terms of the spell that summoned them, limited by the power of the human who cast the summoning.

So they gathered.

And they waited.

Colt, for whatever reason, had constructed the gate so that it could only be unlocked by his pistol. And now, after an eternity of waiting, the metallic clank of the pistol being inserted into the iron gate echoed throughout hell.

The demons screamed and cheered and pushed and shoved. This was it—this was freedom, at last! Free to roam the Earth, free to wreak havoc.

With the squeal of century-old hinges, the gate flew open.

Freedom! Out they crawled, out they ran, out they flew. Some held back, recalling that Colt had also surrounded the gate with an iron pentagram, but Azazel had planned for that—the pentagram had been broken by the human who would lead them. (Another reason, those who had faith pointed out to the doubters, why it was wise for Azazel to conscript a human.)

But there was no human here to lead them. No commands were given, no orders, no instructions, nothing.

They were *truly* free.

The demons scattered to the nine winds, Azazel's plan forgotten as they became drunk with the knowledge that they were unfettered on Earth and could do *whatever they wanted* . . .

ONE

This is the best way to celebrate Christmas and New Year's, Megan Ward thought as she took another gulp of the heavy amber beer that some guy had bought for her, thinking it would get him somewhere.

A resounding bass line made her ribs vibrate, the drums echoing, the guitar slicing through the air like a buzz saw. Megan couldn't remember the name of the power trio that was playing at the Hog's Breath Saloon tonight, but she was enjoying their music. They were a cover band, like most musicians who played the Duval Street bars on Key West, sticking with the usual classic rock favorites. Right now, they were doing "Magic Carpet Ride." The lead singer was a woman with a deep, throaty voice, and she also played the guitar, scorching through the Steppenwolf licks.

They had the volume up loud enough to be

heard on Duval—the Hog's Breath had a large gravel-covered parking lot between it and the Duval Street sidewalk—and so the music could be heard around the giant tree in the center of the fenced-in, open-air bar. Megan was grateful for this for a variety of reasons, not least being it made it easy to ignore the guy who bought her the beer. She didn't turn it down, of course— free booze was free booze, especially on a college student's meager budget—but she wasn't about to let him have his way with her, either. Especially since he spit when he talked, which was just *gross*. Besides, it was just a beer. If he'd bought her a gin and tonic or a screwdriver, then *maybe*, but just a beer? Forget it.

After the human spit-take gave up and moved on to some other chick, Megan actually had one of the small, raised round tables with the high stools to herself. The table was located right between the two bars—the main one in the center of the Hog's Breath and the small one by the parking-lot entrance. That was bound not to last, as there was a steady stream of people in and out of the Hog's Breath on this Saturday night. Some came in from the parking-lot entrance, as Megan had, past that smelly guy who was selling his poetry. Others came from the back entrance on Front Street. She was grateful that she at least didn't have a view of the television behind the smaller bar. A whole bunch of dumb jock types were gathered around watching a college football game.

If Megan had wanted to spend the week after Christmas watching big dumb guys scream over what happened in a football game, she'd have gone back home to Atlanta and her redneck stepfather and stepbrothers.

Mom was all weepy about her little girl not being home for Christmas, but Megan pointed out that she wasn't "her little girl," she was a twenty-two-year-old adult who was trying to get a bachelor's degree at Boston College, and that Mom herself was the only person who'd be in the house that Christmas whom she didn't want to punch in the nose.

Megan didn't blame Mom for remarrying after Dad died in that car accident. Mom had never done the alone thing very well, and a teenage daughter wasn't sufficient, especially since Megan was trying to, y'know, have a *life*. Mom had met Harry in grief counseling, as he was a widower as well, his own wife having died during a liquor-store robbery. He had three sons, and Megan was hard-pressed to decide which one was the worst—Harry Jr., who kept exposing himself to her at every opportunity, Billy, who kept grabbing at her chest and whom she caught once going through her underwear drawer, or little Joey, who set up a web-cam in the bathroom and uploaded a video of Megan showering to the Internet.

Of course, Mom kept insisting that they didn't mean any harm by it, and the boys were just being boys. Since Harry Jr. was twenty-nine and Billy was Megan's age, this didn't really fly, and as for Joey's "prank," Megan had had to hide in her dorm for two months after the shower video had been downloaded by half of BC's campus.

So no going home for Christmas. But there was no way in hell she was staying in Boston, either. Nice place and all, but the winters were just *brutal* for a Georgia gal.

Instead, she came down to Key West. She'd been saving the money she made at the Starbucks on Commonwealth Avenue, managed to get a cheap flight to Key West on the Internet, got a room at a nice bed-and-breakfast right on Duval Street— easy stumbling distance from the bars—and spent her holidays here in a tropical paradise.

Megan loved Key West. Her favorite thing wasn't the bars, the live music, the beautiful weather, the friendly people, the laid-back attitude, the *fantastic* seafood—though she loved all those things—it was the fact that *every single night* on Key West they celebrated the sunset. Every night, folks gathered at the boardwalk and on Front Street and watched the sun go down over the Gulf of Mexico, cheering and celebrating and drinking beer. The boardwalk was filled with vendors and performers, and it was a wonderful party. At first, Megan had thought it to be a onetime thing that she was lucky enough to have arrived in time for, but she soon learned that it was a daily occurrence.

Tonight, she skipped the sunset celebration. She just wanted to sit and listen to music. She'd spent the day playing tourist, going to several of the wrecker museums, the "Little White House," the Hemingway Home and Museum, and the lighthouse, and her feet were *killing* her.

About the only thing that hadn't happened yet was getting laid. Megan had never been good at the boyfriend thing, especially since she kept winding up with boneheads like her stepbrothers. Plus, after the web-cam incident, she couldn't bring herself even to *talk* to most of the guys on campus.

She'd gotten plenty of offers since coming to Key West, but none from anyone she even wanted to be in the same bar with, much less the same bed. All the cute guys she saw were either gay or with someone. For that matter, some of the people who'd hit on her were women, but Megan didn't swing that way, despite the best efforts of some of the other girls in the dorms.

Although if the offers from the men didn't improve soon, she might well consider it.

Still, at least she'd gotten to meet some fun people. Nobody who'd be a friend for life or anything, but fun people to talk to about music and college and life and things. It'd been a different group of people each night, and as far as Megan was concerned, it was part of the fun. She'd consider this trip a success even if she went home alone every night.

The band finished playing "Magic Carpet Ride," and the lead singer said, "We're gonna take a little break. Be back in fifteen!"

Along with most of the rest of the bar's patrons, Megan cheered. (The notable exceptions were the jackasses watching football.) She downed the rest of her beer, then looked around for Liza, the waitress.

"Excuse me, are these seats taken?"

Whirling around, Megan saw an older couple—maybe late forties, early fifties. They were both wearing the Key West "uniform": short-sleeved shirts, shorts, and either flip-flops or sandals. The man who spoke had a slight accent, though Megan couldn't place it—sounded kinda European.

Since they were unlikely to hit on her—though it wouldn't be the strangest thing to happen to her—she said, "No, go ahead."

They shifted the stools so they were right next to each other and facing Megan. The man was very attractive, with olive skin, and what her history professor always referred to as an "aquiline" nose. Megan had no idea why they were called that, except maybe because it sounded more polite than "big." Still, on this guy it worked. He had short, dark, thick hair arranged neatly without obvious evidence of hair-care products.

In contrast, the woman he was with—his wife?—had long dark hair that was laden with such product. She also had huge cheekbones and a perpetual smile. Where the man was rail-thin, the woman was curvy. They actually made kind of a cute couple.

"I am Alberto," the man said with a small smile. "This is my wife, Fedra."

"Thanks for letting us sit," Fedra added with a much bigger smile. "I thought we were gonna have to stand all night." Fedra's accent was more Brooklyn than Europe.

"No problem. I'm Megan."

"Glad to meetcha, Megan."

Alberto asked, "What brings you to Key West?"

Megan didn't really feel like burdening them with her family history, so she just said, "Christmas down here's a lot better than Christmas in Boston, y'know?"

"Oh, I know what you mean," Fedra said, putting her hand on the table. Megan noted the perfectly manicured nails—purple nail polish, with sparkles—and silver rings on most of the fingers. "I can't stand all that snow. And the cold—*maron*."

"What about you guys?" Megan asked.

"We've been spending the past few months traveling," Alberto said. "We had a bit of a life change recently and decided to sell our house and simply *move*."

"Wow." Megan blinked. "That's really cool."

"We're thinkin' a stayin' here for a while, though," Fedra said, leaning forward and speaking in a conspiratorial whisper. "I just *love* the atmosphere here, it's so beautiful." She enunciated that last word as "*byoo*-tee-full."

"Yeah, it's great."

Liza finally came by, a short woman with a deep tan, long brown hair tied back in a sloppy ponytail, and wearing a black shirt with the bar's logo on it. "Another beer, Meg?"

Megan sighed. She hated being called "Meg," but Liza apparently was only willing to use one syllable on a person. She'd been here last night drinking with these three other girls named Christina (whom Liza immediately started calling "Chris"), Melanie ("Mel"), and Elizabeth ("Beth," even though the girl herself preferred to be called "Liz").

Looking at Alberto and Fedra, she said, "And your friends?"

"Can I get a margarita, please?" Fedra said. "*With* salt."

Alberto smiled. "Just a glass of red wine for me, thank you."

"You got it." Liza disappeared into the crowd.

"So you live in Boston, huh?" Fedra asked.

Megan nodded. "I go to college there."

For the next ten minutes or so, Megan told the couple some details about her college career—the usual stupid small-talk answers that she'd given to pretty much everyone she'd met in assorted Duval Street bars over the past few days.

Then the band came back out, and conversation was limited by the noise of the band. Inevitably, they played "Brown-Eyed Girl"—it was impossible to spend an evening on Duval Street without hearing it at *least* three times—as well as a bunch of other hard-rockin' songs.

Alberto surprised her by paying for her drinks. She had three (or was it four?) more beers, and she and the couple kept talking between songs or sometimes by shouting in each other's ears during them. By the time the band finished their second set, she was starting to feel a little woozy. Her feet *still* hurt from the day's excursions, and it might have been time to call it a night. True, it was *hours* before anything would close, but Megan was feeling *really* out of it. She'd been going full tilt since she got here, so maybe it was time to take it easy.

"Look, thanks for the drinks, guys. It was *great* meeting you, but I think I'm gonna turn in early." She pushed back her stool but couldn't get her footing on the ground, and collapsed.

Before she could stop herself, she felt Alberto

grab her arm, steadying her. Despite her body no longer moving, her head swam as the Hog's Breath felt as if it were swirling around like a merry-go-round. "Woooooo boy. Okay, that was bad."

"Where are you staying, Megan?" Alberto asked in his silky voice.

"Uh . . ." She couldn't remember the name of the place. Hell, she suddenly found she couldn't remember her *name. Jesus, what's wrong with me? I only had a couple of beers for Christ's sake.* "It's, uhm, a B&B on Duval—down past Margaritaville."

Fedra said, "I know which one she means. C'mon, honey, let's get you back."

Dimly, Megan registered that several people in the Hog's Breath—Liza among them—were giving her looks of concern as Alberto and Fedra picked her up off the floor and led her toward the back entrance. *Okay, why are we going to the back? That's Front Street. We need to go to Duval, and that means going through the parking lot.* Then again, once sunset was over, Front was comparatively deserted, and maybe the couple thought Megan would prefer fewer crowds.

Right now I just want a bed. And a blanket. And my teddy bear. She still had Mikey Bear, the Toys R Us stuffed bear that her father had given to her the Christmas before he died, and always slept with it. That was another thing that had screwed with her ability to maintain a relationship: All the boys she dated kept laughing at her sleeping with a bear.

Where are we? She couldn't remember. Her feet were shuffling forward, and she felt Alberto on one side, Fedra on the other. It was weird, because Alberto was tall and skinny, and Fedra was short and round, and they were holding her up on different parts of her body. It was like she was listing to the left.

What the heck is going on?

"It's all right, Megan," Alberto was saying. "We will take care of everything."

Fedra was talking, too, but Megan couldn't make it out.

They turned a corner, and Megan realized that she had no idea where they were. She'd only been on Front during sunset, and didn't even know what it would look like without hundreds of people crowding it. She could hear distant sounds, bass lines, shouts, drums, voices—but they were all impossibly far away.

Suddenly, Megan realized that Fedra was still talking. No, she was *chanting. What the hell?* It seemed to be in some foreign language. She caught the occasional word here and there—*invictus, spiritus, phasmae, ligata.*

Why is Fedra chanting in Latin?

They stopped moving. Megan tried to ask what

was going on, but she couldn't make her mouth work.

Fedra kept chanting, louder this time. Megan could only hear the chant, as well as Alberto saying, "Do not worry, Megan—it will be over very soon."

Looking over at Alberto, she saw that he was holding this really nice sparkly knife.

And his eyes had gone all black. *That's such a cool effect.*

The knife moved toward her throat.

Suddenly, the wooziness was gone, and Megan tried to scream, even as the blade touched her throat.

Oh God, no, help me, please, Mom where are you, somebody please, oh God, help!

The scream came out as a bloody gurgle, and she collapsed to the pavement. All she could see was her own blood squirting all *over* the place.

All she could hear were Fedra's chants.

Oh God . . .

The last thing she heard was Alberto's beautiful voice. "It is done."

TWO

"Happy New Year, boys!"

Sam Winchester held up the whiskey glass full of champagne—Bobby Singer didn't have any champagne flutes in his cupboard—and said, "Happy New Year, Bobby."

His older brother, Dean Winchester, just held up his glass and gulped down the champagne.

Staring at the inappropriate glass, Sam said, "You never struck me as the champagne type, Bobby."

Bobby smiled under his beard. "Yeah, I mostly stick to a shot and a beer, but it's New Year's. When I was growin' up, we always had champagne on New Year's while we watched the ball drop. I still make sure to have a bottle in time for the end of December."

Sam looked over at the small television in the living room, which was showing the huge crowd of people in Times Square. Many were wearing silly red hats and glasses shaped like the numerals of the new year, with the middle zeros of 2008 as the eyepieces.

Dean was also staring at the screen, which had just switched to one of the hosts. "Who's the genius who thought replacing Dick Clark with Ryan Seacrest was a *good* idea?"

Swallowing the last of his champagne, Bobby said, "The man had a stroke, Dean."

"I get that—but why replace him with *this* guy? I mean, Dick Clark did *American Bandstand*. All this guy's done is deny that he's gay."

"Well, he *was* on *American Idol*," Sam said.

Fixing his younger brother with a glower that meant that Sam had trod on some beloved piece of pop culture that Dean held dear and Sam didn't care about, Dean said, "Dude, you are *not* equating being on that lame-ass *Star Search* wannabe show with hosting *American Bandstand*, are you?"

Rather than subject himself to one of Dean's rants, Sam didn't answer. "I have a theory, actually."

Dean raised an eyebrow. "Oh, *this* oughtta be good."

"Eventually, the long-term plan is to remove Dick Clark's brain from his own body and place it inside Seacrest's head." He gestured at the screen. "I mean, c'mon, there's plenty of room in there."

Sam was quite proud of the straight face he managed to keep throughout.

Bobby added, in a serious tone, "Y'know, I think I know the spell for that."

Dean finally broke into a laugh.

"Well, it's about time," Sam said. "We're supposed to be celebrating, and you've been a Gloomy Gus."

"'Gloomy Gus'?" Dean shook his head. "Well, thanks for that, Gomer Pyle, but—well, I guess I've just been thinking."

"*That's* always dangerous," Sam said dryly.

"Bite me."

Bobby, now truly serious, asked, "What about, Dean?"

"About 2008, mostly."

Beyond that, Dean didn't elaborate. Sam knew he wouldn't.

This would be Dean's last year on Earth. Unless, of course, Sam could stop it.

Dean had made a deal with a crossroads demon to give up his own life and go to hell after one year, in exchange for said demon bringing Sam back to life. Sam himself had been fatally stabbed by Jake, one of the other kids that the Yellow-Eyed Demon—whose real name was apparently Azazel—had given psychic powers to. All the kids had been gathered into a death-cage match to see who would be worthy of the honor of leading the hordes of hell as they descended upon Earth. Jake and Sam had been the last two.

Thanks to Dean's deal, Sam was able to kill Jake and take the Colt—a pistol that could permanently kill a demon—from him. Dean then used the Colt on Azazel. The price was that Dean only had a year to live.

Sam was bound and determined to find a way to get Dean out of it. He'd shot the crossroads demon with the Colt after she'd told him that she answered to a higher (lower?) demon. He'd even cooperated with Ruby, a demon who seemed to be on the side of good—or, at least, was willing to kill her fellow demons and save Sam's and Dean's asses on several occasions.

But both brothers knew the odds were against Sam's being successful in his quest, and that in all likelihood, come summer, Dean would be sunbathing in hell. And Dean was still treating this as if it were the last year of his life. Sometimes that resulted in behavior that was reckless even by Dean's high standards—Sam tried very hard not to think about some of the things he'd accidentally walked in on Dean doing over the past few months. Sometimes it resulted in melancholy, like what he was displaying now in Bobby's living room.

Turning to Bobby, Sam said, "Thanks for having us, Bobby."

Bobby snorted. "Please. You two are always welcome, you know that."

"It's been quiet for the last week," Sam said. "Ever since we killed those two gods."

"Say that again," Dean said.

Sam frowned. "Say what again?"

"'Ever since we killed those two gods.'" Dean shrugged. "Just gives me a happy, is all. I mean, how often do you get to kill a god, much less two?"

"Two very old, very weak gods," Bobby said. "Only reason the stake worked was 'cause nobody'd worshipped those two for centuries. Gods're only powerful when people believe in 'em. You meet Zeus in a dark alley, he probably couldn't muster up a lightning bolt, but a couple thousand years ago? He'd fry you soon as look atcha."

"Dude," Dean said, "you're harshing my mellow, here."

Sam chuckled. "Wouldn't want that."

"You're right, though, Sammy," Dean said, "good to have a quiet week. Surprised, really—I mean, you'd think there'd be *something* attached to the new year that would get the spirits' panties in a bunch."

"Calendar's arbitrary," Sam said. "It's a human construct. Spirits tend toward more natural things—phases of the moon, solstice, equinox, alignment of the stars, that kind of thing."

"Yeah, I guess." Dean shrugged. "Well, I'll certainly take the time off to drink champagne out of a whiskey glass and watch Ryan Seacrest be boring."

"Hear hear," Sam said, raising his glass.

All three of them downed the last of their champagne.

Dean set the glass down, let out an "Ahh" of satisfaction, then looked at Bobby. "Time to move on to the hard stuff, wouldn't you say?"

Bobby grinned and got to his feet. "Got a bottle of Johnny Walker Black that Ellen got me a good deal on."

Before Bobby could approach the sideboard where he kept the good stuff, the chirp of a cell phone echoed throughout the house.

Immediately, both brothers checked their pockets, but neither Sam's Treo nor Dean's flip-top was the one ringing.

"Hell," Bobby said, "that's your dad's phone."

After John Winchester's death in 2006, Dean had held on to their father's cell phone and kept it charged in case anybody tried to call Dad. Over the months, they'd gotten a case or two that way, but as time went on, the calls tapered off, as word of their father's demise worked its way through the grapevine. After a while (and when the account was about to expire), they left the phone in Bobby's care. He'd renewed the account and passed on what messages there were.

Bobby went into the back room where he kept the phone and picked it up. A moment later, he came back into the living room, holding the phone open. "It's for you," Bobby said, handing the phone to Dean.

Frowning, Dean took it. "Hello?" His hazel eyes widened, and a grin broke out on his face. "Yaphet! How's it hangin', bro?"

Sam stared at Bobby? "Yaphet?"

"A nut job," Bobby said dismissively.

"Really?" Dean was saying. "Okay. Yeah, sure, we'll check it out. It'll be me and my brother this time. *Yeah,* I got a brother. Sam. You'll love Sammy, trust me. Cool. Seeya." Dean closed the phone, still grinning and shaking his head. "Man—that was a blast from the past."

Bobby was staring incredulously at Dean. Sam had to admit that he got that look on his face a lot lately. "You're not actually takin' that hippie burnout seriously, are you?"

Dean shrugged. "Why shouldn't I?"

"Which part of 'hippie burnout' wasn't I clear about?"

"Cah-*mon,* Bobby, I admit, he's a little freaky-deaky, but the guy knows his stuff."

"'The guy' can't even *remember* his stuff."

Having grown tired of needing subtitles for the conversation, Sam raised a hand. "Uh, hello? Can anyone join this discussion?"

Dean turned to look at Sam. "Yaphet the Poet is someone Dad and I met down in Key West while you were at Stanford."

Sam nodded. He knew that Dean and their father had visited Key West at least once before. Sam had gone with Dean to Key West once also, but that was an in-and-out job that hadn't left any time for seeing the island or talking to its denizens. Dean had, Sam recalled, expressed great regret at that, and might have even mentioned this Yaphet guy as part of that.

Dean went on: "He sets up somewhere on Duval Street selling his poetry, and he keeps an eye on the weird stuff." Cutting Bobby off before he could interrupt, Dean said, "And *yes*, he lived through the sixties so good he never left, and he's not always big with the specifics, but if there's something wacky going on in the Keys, he usually knows about it."

"The only wacky thing going on with him," Bobby said, "is his tabacky."

Sam stared blankly at Bobby, as did Dean.

Waving his hand, Bobby said, "You're both too young. Look, I ain't gonna stop you from following up on this, but you might want to wait until a *real* case comes along."

"This might be real, Bobby. Yaphet says that spooks have been on overdrive for the last six months or so."

Sam winced. "Since the Devil's Gate opened?"

Dean nodded. "Mostly it's been more hauntings—Key West has more ghost stories than anyplace this side of New Orleans—plus a weird death. Girl got her throat slit, and there was sulfur on the wound, according to Yaphet."

"Do me a favor, all right?" Bobby said. "Let's check on this 'weird death' from here before you go on down to Florida?"

"Yeah," Dean said, "'cause the absolute *last* thing I want to do is leave the twenty-degree temps here and drive to a place that's famous for sun, warm weather, live music, and partying."

Sam looked at Bobby. "He's got a point."

"I do?" Dean looked at Sam with mock-confusion. "Wait a sec, if you're agreeing with me, something's gotta be wrong."

"Very funny. Look, if it's a real job, we should go. If it isn't, it'll probably be fun."

"No 'probably' about it," Dean said with his biggest this-will-be-*great* smile. "Key West is *always* fun. And this time, we're gonna appreciate it properly."

Bobby threw up his hands. "Fine, do what you want—but I assume you ain't gonna go till morning anyhow, right?"

Dean started to say something, but Sam said, "Right."

"Say what? Sam, if we leave now, we'll make better time."

"We've both been drinking—"

"A glass of champagne and a couple beers. I've driven just fine with more booze in my system. I'll be fine."

Undeterred, Sam went on, even as he admitted to himself that Dean had an enviably high alcohol tolerance. "—plus it's New Year's Eve, so there's bound to be lots of crazy people driving. Let's get a good night's sleep and hit the road in the morning."

"Fine, whatever." Dean got up. "I'm gonna get started on that sleep."

Sam looked up at Bobby, who spoke before Sam could even ask the question. "Go ahead and use the computer."

"Thanks." Bobby's computer was more up-to-date than Sam's laptop, and had a faster processing speed. Sam would dearly have loved to upgrade his machine, but that required funds he just didn't have. They barely survived on credit-card fraud—which, with federal warrants out on both Dean and Sam, was getting increasingly risky—and Dean's ability to hustle pool and win at poker. In fact, just last night, he'd gotten into a high-stakes game. Bobby had lent him the stake money, after a great deal of cajoling, and Dean had won it all back and then some, to the tune of five figures. That would keep them going for a while. Heck, they'd even be able to stay in motels more often, instead of squatting in abandoned houses, as they'd been forced into more than once.

Bobby, of course, had the money because he actually made a living—which enabled him to upgrade his computer every once in a while, too. The Singer Salvage Yard was a thriving business.

As Sam sat down at the keyboard, he was reminded of another reason why he had to find a way to save his brother: Dean was their breadwinner. It was far from the most important reason, and didn't even register ninety-nine percent of the time, but it was there nonetheless. Sam didn't actually have any marketable skills—at least, not any legal ones. He had been less than halfway to a law degree when Dean had come for him at Stanford with the news that Dad had disappeared. The only things he knew how to do were either useless for making money, way outside the law, or in professions (the military, law enforcement) that were likely cut off to him forever.

Of course, illegal behavior wasn't totally out of the question. He was a wanted man in any case, for several felonies, so a few misdemeanors would hardly make a difference. Back at Stanford, he knew a guy who made a good chunk of change writing papers and selling them, and that was certainly an option he could pursue.

But that was a thought for another time. Forcing himself to focus, he made a few online searches and found what he was looking for. A young woman vacationing in Key West named Megan Ward was found with her throat cut on a back street.

Bobby being Bobby, he had several bookmarks to coroners' offices from around the country. Normally, these were highly secure intranets, but Bobby had managed to get through that. Apparently Ash, the now-deceased computer genius who hung out at Harvelle's Roadhouse before it was torched, had performed that feat for him.

Scrolling down, Sam found the Monroe County Medical Examiner's Office site, and was able to track down the M.E. report on the girl's death. Sure enough, her throat was cut—but there was very little blood at the scene, even though her carotid artery had been sliced open, and there was no indication that the body had been moved. The M.E. also noted, as this Yaphet character had, that there was sulfur on the wound, which was odd, as there was no evidence of sulfur anywhere else.

It wasn't odd to Sam, though. Lots of demonic rituals required blood, and demons tended to leave sulfur behind.

"Bobby?" When he came over, Sam pointed at the screen.

"Yeah. All right, I guess the sun shines on a dog's ass once in a while."

Sam set all the pages he'd called up to print on Bobby's laser jet, then stretched his long arms. "All right, I'm gonna hit the hay. Thanks, Bobby."

"No problem. I just hope this isn't a wild-goose chase."

Shrugging, Sam got to his feet. "Worst-case scenario, Dean's cut loose on Key West." He grinned. "Key West may never be the same."

Bobby did not grin back. "Yeah, well, be careful. There's a reason why the place has so many ghost stories. Lotta spiritual energy on that island. If there is a demon that got out of the gate workin' down there, it could be real bad."

Sam nodded. "I know. But we've got the Colt—we'll be all right. Hey, we've already faced down two gods and the seven deadly sins. We should be able to handle this."

Bobby wasn't buying Sam's bravado. Sam had never been very good at it anyhow—that was more Dean's bag. He'd been trying to be more like Dean in preparation for Dean's being gone, but some things just didn't take. Hell, he still was having trouble figuring out what went where under the Impala's hood . . .

Putting a comforting hand on Sam's shoulder, Bobby said, "Keep workin' on it, Sam."

Sam wasn't sure if Bobby was referring to Sam's piss-poor attempt at being cocky or his ongoing attempts to find a way to save Dean. *Maybe it's both,* he thought. He nodded to Bobby, who nodded back. Then he went off to bed.

THREE

Angela O'Shea hadn't always wanted to kill the tourists.

For one thing, she had been one herself. She had come down to Key West for spring break during her sophomore year of college. While her friends were mostly getting drunk and listening to crappy cover bands on Duval Street, she learned how to scuba dive and went parasailing and checked out the museums. She came back the summer after sophomore year, intending to spend just a week.

She had yet to leave.

During her first trip, she'd heard a singer/songwriter do a tune, the refrain of which ran: "Just came down for the weekend, but that was twenty-five years ago." The singer had said that the island was full of people that applied to, and Angela had laughed and thought that to be amusing but ridiculous.

And now she was one of those people.

Having dropped out of college, she had to support herself (her parents were more than happy to pay for college, but that was as far as their generosity went). She had taken on a couple of part-time jobs, including waitressing at one of the bars during the day (when the places were much less crowded and easier to deal with) and being a tour guide for one of the many companies that gave ghost tours at night. Key West was silly with ghost stories, and her job was to take groups of twenty or fewer to allegedly haunted houses and tell exaggerated tales about them.

Angela had figured it to be easy, just working from a script, but it turned out that Cayo Hueso Ghost Tours Inc. liked their tour guides to embellish and perform. Angela had actually done some improv—she'd been a theater major before dropping out—so she started adding her own spins to the stories of Native Americans, wrecker captains, treasure seekers, and artists of various stripes whose shades allegedly haunted the island.

The job started out fine. It seemed like there were always one or two idiots in every tour group, and always one or two rude assholes who complained about everything and didn't tip. At first, she was willing to put up with that, but five months later, it hadn't gotten any better. Not to mention the self-proclaimed skeptics who tried to "disprove" what she was saying, thus ruining the fun for everyone else.

It wasn't like anybody *really* believed this stuff. Well, okay, that wasn't true, lots of people did, so why ruin their fun? It wasn't like some grad student dork was gonna change their minds . . .

Today she had the worst of all worlds. They started out at the old Lipinski place on Eaton Street, which had been purchased by CHGT after old Mr. Lipinski went into the sanitarium. The house had been in his family since the nineteenth century, but they had to sell the place to pay for the old guy to go to the nuthouse. And it was the center of one of the stories anyhow, so the company bought it and put a gift shop in what used to be the sitting room, but otherwise left the house intact—including the room in the turret for the doll.

As she took the group up the winding stairs to the turret, one overweight man wearing a thick sweatshirt and jeans said, "Nobody told me there'd be *stairs*. I can't take a lot of *stairs*."

Five months' practice was the only thing that kept Angela from saying, "If you ate a salad once in a while, you'd be in better shape." Instead, she asked a question that the man's wardrobe had already answered: "Your first day in Key West, sir?"

"Why—yes. How'd you know?"

The only people stupid enough to wear a sweatshirt and jeans are the ones who just got here. "You'll find that many people walk on the island. Everything's pretty close together, for the most part. You might want to consider one of the pedi-cabs." They were always told to mention the pedi-cabs, since the brother of CHGT's owner ran one of the pedicab companies. Technically, she was supposed to give the company name, but she never did that, as it struck her as unethical.

When they got to the top of the wooden stairs, which had creaked and groaned under the weight of so many people, everyone bunched in the doorway at the top of the steps. Angela removed the top hat that was part of her work clothes. Normally, Angela was strictly T-shirt and shorts, but for work, she put on the big black top hat, the black taffeta skirt, the black stockings, the white button-down shirt and black vest, the multiple black bracelets, and the big stompy boots. She also overdid the eyeliner and put on black lipstick. She had resisted Goth-ifying herself at first, but the boss insisted, and she did notice that the tourists responded to her better when she looked like a Marilyn Manson fan.

Angela stepped inside the small room, hunched over so she wouldn't hit her head on the ceiling. The room at the top of the turret really could only accommodate a small child. She indicated the undersized furniture—the man in the sweatshirt probably couldn't fit his fat ass in the sofa—and said, "This is where Raymond lives. Raymond is a doll." Angela moved aside so everyone could get a better view. Besides the small couch in the center of the room, there was an end table that looked like a coffee-cup saucer with four legs attached to it (on top of which was a dinky desk lamp that could only accommodate a Christmas-tree light, providing the only illumination and making the room spookier), a rocking chair that looked like it belonged to a three-year-old, and an easy chair.

It was on that chair that Raymond sat.

Sweatshirt man wiped sweat from his large brow, and said, "That's the *ugliest* thing I ever saw! God, Marcia, isn't that the ugliest thing you ever saw?"

The almost-as-overweight woman with him just nodded sagely, carrying the look of a woman who'd long since learned to just stay quiet and under the radar. Angela's mother had that look; being married to Angela's father did that to a person. Her dad belonged in the same insane asylum as old Mr. Lipinski . . .

And fat man wasn't wrong in any event—Raymond was a very ugly doll, looking more like a monkey than the small child it was supposed to represent. It wore a striped shirt under its round head and fat face and oversized jaw.

"Raymond was a gift from a Bahamian housekeeper in 1904 to a young boy who lived here. It was his favorite toy—but it got him into trouble. The boy was always a good child, until he received Raymond, at which point he became a *terrible* prankster." She hesitated, having long since learned the value of the dramatic pause. "Or so everyone *thought*. You see, the young man insisted, to the point of tears, that it was Raymond who'd knocked over the priceless vase, Raymond who fed spoiled meat to the dogs, Raymond who tracked mud into the house when it rained, Raymond who set the Christmas tree on fire." She only added that last one around this time of year. That hadn't been part of the story, but she remembered reading somewhere that people used to put actual candles on their Christmas trees, so it struck her that fires had to be fairly common, and it was the kind of thing a kid—or a doll possessed by a ghost, ha-ha—might do.

An acne-festooned teenager wearing a Van Halen T-shirt said, "What, and people *believed* that? I mean, *duh,* it was the kid!"

"Maybe it was." Another dramatic pause. "And maybe it wasn't!"

Angela put her hat back on and led them down the creaky stairs. Once, Angela had asked why they didn't replace the stairs, but her boss pointed out that creaky stairs in a haunted house is a *good* thing.

Jonathan *still* hadn't shown up to run the gift shop, like usual, so Angela locked up the house and hoped he deigned to arrive by the time the tour was over. She hated having to run the gift shop after doing the whole tour.

Over the following hour, she took the group out onto the early-evening streets to each of the other six houses on the tour, and described some of the hauntings. Between each one, the fat man complained about how much *walking* and *standing* they were doing, and don't they get a *break*? At each one, a pair of older women who appeared to be sisters hung on Angela's every word, gasping in all the right places and saying that that was amazing. Right after that, the kid with the acne would come up with what he thought was a logical and scientific—and possibly accurate, not that Angela cared—explanation of each haunting, earning him a dirty look from the two sisters.

By the time she got to the story of Captain Naylor, she was about ready to kill all of them. The sisters' simpering approval was almost as bad as Acne Boy's channeling of Dana Scully—and both of them were a treat compared to the fat man.

"Captain Terrence Naylor owned this house during his life as a wrecker captain. During the nineteenth century, one of the most lucrative businesses on Key West was the wreckers. Ships and boats were regularly getting damaged on the reefs, and wreckers would go out and do rescue and salvage. A lot of the houses on this island were built by wrecker captains with the money they made."

"That's *awful*," the fat man said. "Profiting on people's suffering like that."

Angela ground her teeth. That was the other thing she got regularly, people who were outraged at the wreckers' actually making a living. "They were performing a service—and it was a very specific and well-regulated service. They weren't profiting on misery any more than firefighters do. Without wreckers, a lot more people would've died out on the sea."

The fat man didn't look convinced, so Angela went back to ignoring him and telling them about how Captain Naylor had been haunting the house since he died in 1872, and how to this day, guests at the Naylor House Bed and Breakfast would hear the captain's voice in the night . . .

"Prob'ly just the wind," Acne Boy said. "Tropical breezes, all'a trees—plus all'a live music right 'round the corner on Duval. Only really really stupid people'd believe that was a ghost." That last was said while looking right at the sisters.

The Naylor House was right across the street from the Lipinski House, so the tour ended when Angela walked them across Eaton Street and stood under a streetlamp. "Thank you all for coming to our tour." Glancing at the front door, she saw that it was unlocked, and the display lights in the gift shop were on, so obviously Jonathan had materialized. "The gift shop is available, and I hope you all enjoy your stay in the Keys."

Some of the group didn't bother coming inside—

including, thank God, Acne Boy—while others went in to browse the items in the shop. They sold books about the island, about the folklore, about some of the famous people and historical events of the Keys, and so on. There were also maps, post-cards, gift cards, CDs by local artists, and various silly *tchotchkes* that tourists always liked to buy for whatever stupid reason.

While folks browsed, Angela walked up to the desk and glowered at the pale, long-haired, bearded young man with the beer gut already sticking out from under his too-small T-shirt. At least he'd remembered to bathe this morning. He had his nose in a gaming magazine that had an orc or something on the cover.

"'Bout *time* you showed up," she said.

"What?" Jonathan said defensively without looking up from the magazine. "I knew you wouldn't be done with these guys until seven."

"What if I finished early? Or what if one of them wanted to buy something at the start? You're *supposed* to be here at six."

Jonathan shook his head. "Whatever."

Sighing, Angela looked around and made a beeline for the fat man, who was with his wife looking at the Florida license plates with people's names on them. He was holding up a license plate emblazoned with the name TERRY. "We should get this for our niece."

His wife frowned. "Doesn't she spell it with an I?"

"What do you mean?"

"It's 'Terri,' with an I. She don't spell it like that, with a Y."

"What difference does *that* make?"

Angela walked up to him. "Thanks again for coming on the tour," she lied. "If you have any questions, don't hesitate to ask Jonathan over there."

"Oh, thank you, I will," the fat man said.

Yes. "Good."

A pair of young men who appeared to be a couple, and who'd been blessedly silent during the tour, came up to Angela.

"Excuse me, Angela?" one of them said.

"Yes?"

"I think I left my bracelet up in Raymond's room."

The other one made a *tsk* noise. "Dammit, Paulie, I *told* you to get that clasp fixed, but do you listen?"

"Oh shut *up*, Mario, I'm just—"

Mario held up a hand. "Fine, fine, *don't* listen to me, I don't know *anything*."

Angela put on her best smile. "I can run up and check for you."

"Could you please?" Paulie said, his wide eyes and hopeful smile giving him a look of gratitude. "That would be so great. It's a silver bracelet with a Celtic knotwork pattern on it."

"No problem." She regretted the risk of not

being there when the fat man descended upon Jonathan, but knowing the man in question, Angela'd probably still hear whatever he harangued the dork with from upstairs.

Going up the winding staircase, she opened the door to find that the furniture had been rearranged. The tiny couch was now against the wall, the rocker had been rotated ninety degrees, and the easy chair was facing the window.

Raymond was also on the couch.

Right on the threshold was an unclasped silver bracelet that had a very lovely Celtic knotwork pattern etched all around it. Smiling, Angela picked it up and walked back downstairs, the wood creaking under her heavy boots.

Once the tourists had paid for their goodies and left (Mario and Paulie both expressing gratitude for her retrieving the missing bracelet, Paulie promising Mario that *this time* he'd get the damn clasp fixed), Jonathan and Angela were alone in the house—at least until the eight o'clock group started to trickle in.

"What's with the redecorating in Raymond's room?" she asked Jonathan, who had gone back to his gaming magazine.

"What're you talkin' 'bout?" he asked without raising his head.

"Raymond's room. You rearranged all the furniture."

Finally, Jonathan looked up. "Angie, the hell're you *talkin'* about? I just got here five minutes 'fore you did. Barely had time to unlock the place an' turn the lights on 'fore you guys came all bargin' in. I ain't been upstairs."

"Then who rearranged the furniture?"

"Hell if *I* know." Jonathan looked back down at the magazine.

Shaking her head, Angela went back up the winding stairs. *This is seriously messed up.* The stairs seemed to be creaking extra loudly this time.

Stop it, it's just your imagination. Jonathan's probably lying. Or maybe Stella or Gene came in while the tour was going on. That'd be just like them.

When she got back to the top of the stairs, she pushed the door slowly open, and it creaked even louder than the stairs had. Hating the sound of it, she pushed harder, throwing the door all the way open with a crash against the brick wall of the turret.

Angela stared at the room. It looked like it had when she came up for Paulie's bracelet.

But the doll was gone.

She walked over to the sofa, which had a small indentation on the spot where Raymond *had* been sitting. *So how the hell did it move?* The only door to the house that hadn't been sealed shut was the front door, a security measure that had been put in to safeguard the merchandise and cash register in the gift shop. The house wasn't that big—Angela would've seen somebody try to sneak upstairs in the time between her retrieval of the bracelet and now.

So who took the stupid doll?

Angela nearly jumped out of her skin as the wooden door slammed shut with a louder crash than it had made when she threw it open.

"Okay, Jonathan, this just stopped being funny." She stomped over to the door, grabbing the handle and yanking on it—and almost wrenched her shoulder. She'd easily opened and shut the door any number of times since starting this job, but now it wouldn't budge.

After yanking on it a few more times, she started slamming her palms against it. "Hey! Jonathan! Open the damn door!"

Reaching into the pocket of her vest, she pulled out her cell phone. She'd had enough of this crap.

Flipping it open, the words NO SERVICE were emblazoned across the top of the screen.

What the hell? She'd never had a problem with cell reception except sometimes when it rained. Certainly, the house wasn't a dead zone. Hell, she'd had a half-hour conversation with her now-ex-boyfriend in this very room a month ago.

Angrily closing the phone, she looked around the room—

—and saw Raymond standing on the end table.

The little lamp was on the floor, even though Angela had neither heard nor seen it being moved.

"All right, this is so *totally* messed up. If somebody doesn't—"

Raymond launched through the air right at Angela. Too stunned at this impossible thing happening, she didn't duck out of the way despite instincts honed from two semesters' worth of self-defense classes back at college.

The doll's impact knocked her backward, her head colliding with the door, her hat tumbling to the floor. Her vision swam, and she felt suddenly nauseous, even as she wondered how a hundred-year-old doll stuffed with straw could knock her down, much less jump.

Raymond's cloth hands, with no fingers, clamped the sides of her head. Angela tried to blink the spots out of her eyes and tried also to speak, to ask what was going on, but it just came out as gibberish. The doll rammed the back of her head into the thick wooden door again.

Her nausea was overwhelming. There were two Raymonds in front of her now, swirling about and never changing that same simian expression it always had, but those dinky little arms kept their grip on her head and slammed it against the wall again and again and again . . .

FOUR

Sam watched the setting sun paint the sky over the Gulf of Mexico a magnificent orange and purple.

Dean drove their fully restored 1967 Chevrolet Impala across the Seven Mile Bridge, a long stretch of U.S. Route 1 that linked Key Vaca and Little Duck Key. They had driven down from Bobby's on major highways for as far as they could, until Interstate 95 ended at the southern tip of mainland Florida.

From there, it was down Route 1, or the Overseas Highway as it was called on this stretch, which was the only road that linked all of the Florida Keys together. The last time they'd come here, it was after sunset, and they'd done what they had to—clearing a poltergeist from a motel—and left the following morning for another job.

They'd been driving for two straight days to cover the two thousand miles between the

Singer Salvage Yard in South Dakota and the Florida Keys. Key West itself was the southernmost point in the continental U.S. Rather than bother with a motel for New Year's Night, they slept in shifts while the other drove down the various interstates through Iowa, Missouri, Illinois, Kentucky, Tennessee, and Georgia, before finally getting to Florida, then having to drive all the way down its peninsula. They arrived right as the sun was going down on the second of January.

"Great sunset, ain't it?" Dean said.

"Yeah. This whole part of the drive is nice, actually. We spend so much time on interstates, it's nice to have a scenic drive for a change."

"First time Dad and I came down here, he was driving, and I was like you—starin' out the window like a dog."

Sam chuckled. "So this is why you were so hot to come back down here? So we could roll down the car windows?"

"Among other things." Dean was smiling widely and turned up the volume on the radio so it could be heard over the wind whipping into the Impala from outside. He'd found a Miami classic rock station, and it was playing "Long Time" by Boston. "Duval Street is like a more laid-back version of Bourbon Street. Lots of bars, lots of live music, lots of partying."

"And lots of ghosts."

"Yeah." They got to the end of the bridge, and the scenery was now tall grass and the occasional gas station.

Sam shifted his lanky frame in the seat. "It's also kind of a tourist trap. Where we gonna find a motel we can, y'know, afford?"

"Not a problem in the least. See, the job Dad and I did down here involved chasing off a nixie that was using one of the bed-and-breakfasts as a feeding ground. The owner was sufficiently grateful that she said we could stay for free anytime we were on the island."

Sam nodded, grateful. "Good thing. I think we blew through the last of the poker winnings when we filled up this morning." Of course, last time the job had been *in* a motel, so they had to stay there to deal with the poltergeist.

Dean let out a long breath. The recent hike in gas prices had played merry hell with their lives and was one of the main reasons why squatting in abandoned houses had become a necessary alternative to motels on occasion. The Impala was all Sam and Dean had. While they were welcome at Bobby's and it was a sanctuary for them, it wasn't their home. The Impala, though, was.

But this home needed feeding. Bobby had been kind enough to gas them up for free before they left, but good gas mileage was not among the Impala's virtues, and they'd had to fill it up several times since departing South Dakota.

As they got farther south on the Overseas Highway, traffic started to pile up a bit. It was a two-lane road—one lane going north, the other south—so everyone had to go as fast as the slowest car on the road, a situation that usually made Dean cranky. However, he was taking it in stride. *This must be a fun place,* Sam thought with a small smile. And he'd take whatever he could get of Dean being happy.

They went over one final bridge on Stock Island and made a right turn on the other side, now on Key West proper. They passed several large hotels and malls. It looked surprisingly suburban to Sam, but then Dean made a right onto a large side street, and suddenly it looked like he expected: wooden houses, pastel colors, eighteenth- and nineteenth-century architecture. This was Old Town, the downtown area of Key West, the part that had the tourist traps, the beaches, and the bars.

Dean then turned left onto Eaton Street. They passed more houses, a few municipal buildings, and eventually pulled up to a house that was behind a wrought-iron gate and several large trees. Across the street was a house with a turret that had a sign that read CAYO HUESO GHOST TOURS.

Sam climbed out of the Impala and felt his knees crack as he straightened them for the first time in what seemed like years. *You'd think my knees would be used to sitting in a car for hours at a time,* he thought dolefully.

Walking through the gate, Sam and Dean walked down a short tree-lined brick path to a set of wooden steps up to a lovely porch, complete with swing. The front door was wide open, and Sam entered to see a roomful of bookcases and sea-related memorabilia. The far wall had a huge painting of a sailing ship, with a large harpoon mounted horizontally over it. To the left, there were two photos of the coastline at sunset between the bookcases.

To the right was a desk and a door to a hallway, as well as a large anchor abutting the wall. However, nobody was sitting at the desk.

"Hello?" Dean called out as they entered.

In response, a giant gray-and-white sheepdog came bounding in, tongue hanging from its mouth. Stopping in front of Dean, it barked.

Breaking into a huge grin, Dean said, "Oh man, Snoopy? That you?" Dean knelt and started scratching the dog on the back of its neck. In response, the sheepdog rested its front paws on Dean's knees and started licking his hand.

Sam found himself forced to ask, "The dog's *really* named Snoopy?"

"Yup. He was just a little puppy last time I was here. You've gotten all big, haven't you?"

"Whoever named him *does* know that Snoopy was a beagle, right?"

A voice came from the door to the hallway. "He had the name when we got him, and it's the only name he responds to."

Looking up, Sam saw a very short, very attractive young woman with surprisingly pale skin for someone who lived on a tropical island, curly red hair that was tied back into a ponytail, numerous freckles, and sea-green eyes. Like most of the people Sam had seen walking around on the drive over, she was wearing a T-shirt—it was emblazoned with a black-and-white line drawing of this house along with the words NAYLOR HOUSE BED & BREAKFAST—and shorts and flip-flops.

The redhead continued: "I wanted to rename him Bustopher Jones, but he wouldn't come when you called that, and he *does* come for Snoopy. So what're you gonna do?"

Dean stood upright, leaving Snoopy to run around his legs a few times. "How you been, Nicki?"

Nicki embraced Dean, and said, "Good to see you again, Deano. Knew it was you when I saw that boat of yours parked outside. You should pull it into the driveway, you can't keep it on the street overnight." She broke the embrace and gazed up and down at Sam. "Who's the big guy?"

"I'm, uh, 'Deano's' brother, Sam," he said, holding out his hand.

"Oh, *you're* Sammy, huh?" Nicki said, returning the handshake.

"Uh, yeah," Sam replied, suddenly nervous.

Sporting a wide grin that showed perfect teeth, Nicki said, "I heard *all* about you last time Deano blew through the Keys."

"Well, don't believe a word he said. I'm actually a nice person."

Nicki glanced over at Dean. "Yeah, he's your brother, all right."

Dean, who had gone back to petting Snoopy, much to the sheepdog's delight, said, "Yup. Can't live with him, can't shoot him."

"So you guys need a room?"

Sam nodded.

"Actually, you're in luck—I can give you three."

Frowning, Dean said, "Three? Why would we—"

"Uh," Sam said quickly, "we only need two. Our father, he—" Sam glanced at Dean, who had his patented awkward expression on.

Nicki's face fell. "Oh no—oh, geez, I'm sorry. One of the spooks got him?"

"Something like that," Dean said quietly.

"Damn. I really liked Johnny, he was sweet."

There are many adjectives Sam would have used to describe John Winchester. *Sweet* didn't make the cut. But he said only, "Anyhow, we're fine with one room. We don't want to take up too much space."

"It's not a problem. If you were here last week, it'd be one thing, we had a full house, but everybody checked out yesterday. We just got a couple in three, and the rest of the place is empty. Typical for right after New Year's, really—especially when you add in a double homicide across the street."

Sam shot his brother a look. "Double homicide?"

Nicki nodded. "Yeah, two of the people who worked at the ghost-tour company." She pointed at the house with the turret. "Someone found 'em with their heads bashed in. Nice folks, too. Girl's name was Angela, and the guy was Jonathan. We're the last stop on the tour, and sometimes we feed 'em."

"Is that place supposed to be haunted, too?" Dean asked.

"Yeah—that's why the tour company bought it. I'm guessin' that's why you two are here?"

Normally, Sam and Dean would be circumspect, but Nicki knew what they really did for a not-living. So Dean said, "Part of it, yeah. You know where Yaphet's set up these days?"

"You'll prob'ly find him in the Hog's Breath parking lot. If not, try outside the Bull." Walking around to behind the desk, Nicki opened a drawer and pulled out two key chains, each of which had two keys on them. "You guys have any bags?"

"Everything's in the car," Dean said. "We'll fish it out when we park it."

"Okee dokee. Come with me."

Nicki led them through the door to the hall-way. Sam couldn't help but notice two things: one, Nicki's shorts were *very* short, and her rear end moved quite provocatively in them as she walked; and two, Dean *wasn't* noticing that. Generally lacking in subtlety where attractive members of the opposite sex were concerned, Dean's lack of reaction to their host's hotness was tremendously out of character.

As they turned a corner and went out a doorway and down three small steps to the outdoors, Nicki said, "Hey, girl, look who's back?"

Sam followed Nicki and Dean out the door and saw a huge garden, filled with colorful flowers, giant trees, and several comfortable-looking white wicker chairs. In one sat a tall, broad-shouldered woman with short brown hair, a dark tan, half a dozen rings in one ear (and none in the other), plus one in her nose. Wearing a brown tank top and black shorts, she leapt to her bare feet and grinned widely. "Deany-baby!" she cried in a booming voice that seemed to echo off the trees. "You're back!"

Sam looked at his brother. "'Deany-baby'?"

"Shut *up*," Dean muttered, then smiled, and said, "How you been?"

Nicki slid her arm around the woman in a very affectionate manner that suddenly explained *why*

Dean wasn't hitting on Nicki. "And this is Dean's brother Sam. Sam, this is my partner, Bodge."

"Pleased to meet you."

"Likewise!"

"I gave 'em six and seven," Nicki said.

Nodding, Bodge said, "Cool!" Her voice seemed permanently turned up to eleven.

Extricating herself from her partner, Nicki led them down a brick path through the trees to a pair of small two-story houses of the same design as the main one. Each had a room on the ground floor, a wooden staircase up to a porch that led to another room on the second floor. Sam could see that the room also had only one double bed, which precluded the pair of them sharing. They'd shared beds in the past, but it was never a good night's sleep, as Sam tended to sprawl, and Dean tended to kick.

"The two rooms in this bungalow are yours," Nicki said.

"I'll take the top floor," Sam said, figuring the stairs would be good exercise.

Nicki handed him the key chain that had the number 6 on it. "Here you go. The silver key opens the door up front—we lock it around ten or so, so if you come in later than that, you'll need the key to get in. The other one opens your room up."

"Thanks." Sam pocketed the chain and looked at Dean. "We should get our stuff."

"Yeah." Dean took his own key, and Nicki went with them back to the main house.

After pulling the Impala into the driveway adjacent to the Naylor House, Dean got out and just stood for a moment, closing his eyes and feeling the tropical sun on his face.

Intellectually he knew it was the same sun that had been shining in South Dakota, but it sure as hell didn't *feel* like it. Up north, the sun was just taunting him, teasing with warmth while the wind chill sliced through him. Here, though, the sun was inviting, welcoming.

Glad I had a reason to come back here before it's all over.

Dean sighed and went to the trunk to join Sam in unloading the small overnight bags that contained changes of clothes, toiletries, and other odds and ends. How Dean felt about his impending doom varied from day to day—*hell, from hour to freakin' hour*—but at this particular second, he was okay with it. He'd saved a lot of lives, done a lot of good, and kept his brother safe.

That was the most important thing. Sammy had to be kept safe. When Mom was killed by the yellow-eyed bastard, Dad had handed Sam's tiny six-month-old self to Dean and given an order: "Take your brother outside as fast as you can— don't look back. Now, Dean, *go!*"

It sometimes felt like that order had defined Dean's life. Now it was defining his death.

The first time he'd been to Key West, he'd met this fantastic girl at Captain Tony's. That had been a night to remember, especially after Nicki and Bodge had turned down his perfectly reasonable request for a threesome. Dean couldn't remember the girl's name, but he did recall with perfect clarity the curve of her breasts, the smell of the herbal shampoo she used mixed with sweat, and the taste of her lips. She was the sister or cousin or something of the band that was playing at Captain Tony's, just down for two weeks before going back to Alabama with the band.

Dean decided that he had to go back to Captain Tony's at some point. It was obviously a good-luck charm.

He and Sam trudged back through the main house to the backyard. Dean realized that he hadn't seen the parrot that lived in the garden, and he wondered if it was hiding.

"Once we get settled," Dean said to Sam, as they approached the small house where Nicki had put them, "we should go across the street, see what we can turn up."

"Sure thing, Deano," Sam said with a chuckle.

"I will kill you with my hands," Dean said. He had forgotten that Nicki and Bodge insisted on calling everyone by some kind of cutesy nickname, and *of course* Sammy was giving him a hard time about it.

Then again, they were likely to come up with something for him before long, and then Dean would have his revenge.

Sam went upstairs, the wood creaking under his lanky frame.

Dean dug the key chain out of his pants pocket and slid the key into the large sliding door. Pushing it aside, he entered the room, which was a bit stuffy. While it was much warmer than it was at Bobby's, it was cool by Florida standards, so opening the window did the trick. Last time, Dean and Dad had been here in summertime, and the air conditioner was absolutely necessary.

The room had a double bed with a white wicker headboard of the same style as the garden furniture, which suited Dean fine. This time, he'd be able to bring someone home without having to worry about disturbing his traveling companion. The walls and carpet were a matching pastel, and there were seascapes hanging on the wall, as well as a ship's wheel.

Reaching up, Dean yanked on the chain that started the ceiling fan going, and he left the big sliding door open but closed the screen door to keep the bugs out. He considered warning Sam about the mosquitoes, then decided it would be more fun for him to learn that lesson his own self.

"What in blazes are you doing in my house?"

Whirling around, Dean saw a man wearing a blue cap, a blue jacket, and white pants. Dean also clearly saw the wall behind the man.

In all his years of hunting, Dean had encountered many a spirit. Few of them had ever been this—well, *coherent*.

"Uh—"

"I asked you a question, young man. This is my abode, and I wish to know what you're doing in it!"

"And you are?"

"Captain Terrence Naylor, of course! Now answer my blasted question!"

FIVE

Greg Mitchell had kept telling his wife Krysta that Key West would be the perfect place to spend New Year's. It wasn't until they'd been there for three days that she'd admitted that he was right.

As a happily married man, Greg was used to never being told that he was right about something, so he considered Krysta's admission to be a major victory.

Her skepticism was born out of Key West's not being the best place in the world to go scuba diving. They'd dove in Hawaii and in Turks and Caicos and in the Cook Islands and in Papua New Guinea, and any number of other locations that had far better diving than the Keys could offer.

But what Key West had that those places didn't was the excellent night life. Every night, they went to a different Duval Street bar, drank good beer, and listened to good music. One night, they even did karaoke, the pair of them "singing" both "Time of My Life" and "Paradise by the Dashboard Light."

Today, they had been all set to take another dive, but the wind was fierce, and the water too choppy for diving. Luckily, the dive shop had called them at the hotel and told them so they had time to make other plans for the day.

They decided to be touristy and see various sights. "Wanna go to the Little White House?" Greg asked, as they sat at the foot of the bed in their hotel room at the Hyatt on Front Street.

"What about the Hemingway House?"

"I guess. I mean, it's just Hemingway." Even as he said the words, Greg wished he could have taken them back.

"'Just' Hemingway? Ernest Hemingway is the greatest American writer!"

"Only if you don't count every other American writer." They'd been having this argument for years. In fact, they had it before they started dating, as they'd first met in an American literature class in college where the subject came up. (The professor, of course, was on *her* side, but most of the class was on his.)

Krysta opened her mouth as if to say something, closed it, then held up a hand. "We're not doing this. Look, whatever you think of his writing, he lived here, and there's this great museum dedicated to him. *And* it's full of cats."

Greg blinked. "Cats?"

Nodding, Krysta said, "Yup. A whole mess of them. And they're all six-toed."

"You're kidding!" Greg felt his eyes grow wide. "Oh, that's *great*. Polydactyl cats are just *cool*." A cat person his entire life, his and Krysta's apartment back home in Lawrence, Kansas, currently held three felines, who were being cared for by Greg's sister while their providers were on vacation.

Shaking her head, Krysta got up and moved toward the door, grabbing her large black Coach bag on the way. The expensive purse didn't really track with the T-shirt, shorts, and mesh sandals she was wearing, but Krysta insisted that she needed something big enough to carry all her stuff, and Greg had long since given up trying to argue.

"Why can't you just say 'six-toed' cats like everyone else?" she asked.

"See, this is what I'm talking about," Greg said as he grabbed the battered old Kansas City Royals cap he'd had since he was a kid and followed her out. "Hemingway was the kind of writer who would use 'six-toed' instead of 'polydactyl', but 'polydactyl' is a perfectly acceptable word to use for anyone who's remotely educated."

Closing the door behind them—if you didn't pull it shut, it didn't always close all the way, and they had valuables in there—they proceeded down the hall to the elevator. Krysta started rummaging in her purse while saying, "Yeah, but the term's imprecise. All 'polydactyl' means is having more fingers or toes than usual. 'Six-toed' means precisely what the cats in the Hemingway House are: six-toed. Aha!" That last was when she finally dug her sunglasses out of the huge purse.

Greg hated it when Krysta wore the sunglasses, because they covered her amazing blue eyes. They had come out of the English class not liking each other, but met again the next semester at a party held in a mutual friend's dorm suite. She'd changed her hair color, so he didn't recognize her, and started hitting on the woman with the amazing blue eyes, not discovering until they'd been up all night talking (well past the point where the party had fizzled out) that she was his nemesis from the American Lit class. Her eyes were like pools of moonlight, and she only groaned a little when he'd said that out loud the first time.

Tapping the down button for the elevator with his right knuckle, Greg said, "I thought we weren't having this argument."

"We aren't—this is an argument about you being a pretentious academic twit, not an argument about the relative merits of Hemingway's writing."

"I could've sworn I tied this to Hemingway," he said with a smile.

"Yes," Krysta said tartly, "and I ignored that in

favor of calling you a twit. I *said* I wasn't having this argument."

Shaking his head and laughing, he said, "I love you."

Her blue eyes twinkled just as she put the sunglasses on over them. "I love you, too."

It was a short, pleasant walk down Front to Whitehall, then down Whitehall several blocks until they reached Olivia Street, passing several houses, restaurants, and such on the way—not to mention one of the entrances to the Little White House, which had been Harry S Truman's preferred vacation spot while he was president, eschewing Camp David (which back then was called Shangri-La). Across the street from the Hemingway House was the giant lighthouse. Looking up at the huge cylindrical structure, Greg said, "We should go there after Hemingway."

"Um, okay."

Shooting his wife a look at her hesitant tone, Greg asked, "What?"

"Well, you know there's no elevator, right? You have to *walk* all the way up to the top of that thing."

"Yeah, so?" Greg said indignantly, not liking the implication.

"All right, but when we're halfway up and you're all winded from hauling the Buddha Belly up all those stairs, don't come crying to me."

Self-consciously patting his potbelly—which Krysta had affectionately dubbed "the Buddha Belly" two years ago—he said, "I thought you *liked* the Buddha Belly."

"I love it, my sweet, but it's an impediment to stair-climbing."

"Bah. And fooey. I will climb the stairs, and I will laugh at your mockery of my fitness."

"Assuming you can breathe, sure," Krysta said with a smile and a peck on his cheek.

Said peck did not mollify him. "C'mon, let's go look at the paean to an overrated author."

Krysta stuck out her tongue, then proceeded to the ticket booth in front of the brick wall that surrounded the house. Behind the booth was an ivy-covered gate, currently open.

After paying the entrance fee to a bored-looking young woman in the booth who looked put out by them interrupting her reading of *Entertainment Weekly,* they proceeded through the gate and up the stairs to the house. A smiling young man with small eyes, a big nose, and crooked teeth greeted them as they approached. "Hello! Welcome to the Hemingway Home and Museum! Is this your first time?"

There was no one else around. Greg had noticed that there were fewer people on the streets this morning than there had been other mornings, and he attributed that to it being the day after New

Year's—which was part of why they'd planned for their stay to extend past the holiday. "Yes, it is."

"My name's David, and I'll be running the tour, which starts at fifteen minutes past the hour. Until then, I'll be happy to answer any questions you might have." As if anticipating the first one, he continued: "The house was originally built in 1851 by Asa Tift, who was a marine architect and a wrecker. Ernest Hemingway made this his home in 1931."

Krysta asked, "Why is there a brick wall around the house? Security?"

Greg wasn't interested in that—he was looking for the cats, and was surprised not to see any.

"After a fashion," David said in response to Krysta's query. "Originally there was a simple chain-link fence around the property, but Mr. Hemingway wanted privacy from the people who would stare at the house. Mr. Hemingway was quite the celebrity, and Key West is a much more casual locale than, say, Hollywood, so—"

"Where are the cats?"

Suddenly David got nervous. "Er—I'm afraid— you see—"

"What is it?" Greg asked.

"Are you all right?" Krysta added, concern in her voice.

Palming sweat off his forehead, David said, "It's nothing, I just—anything else about Mr. Hemingway you'd like to know?"

"Are the cats really descendants of the polydactyl he had?"

Krysta put in, "My husband is more a cat person than a Hemingway person, I'm afraid."

David winced. "Oh, I wish you hadn't said that."

"What? Why—" Suddenly, Greg felt a hand grab his shoulder. Whirling around, he saw—

Nobody. But he still felt the hand.

A voice cried out, echoing off the brick walls and vibrating within Greg's ribs, seeming to come from everywhere at once. "Get out! Get out, get out, *get out*!"

The hand pushed Greg, sending him stumbling down the stairs toward the gate. Greg tried to get his feet under him, but couldn't get solid purchase, and fell to the ground. He winced in pain as his right arm struck the pavement.

"Oh my God, *Greg*!" Krysta ran to him, kneeling down next to him. "Are you all right?"

Greg clambered to a sitting-up position and looked at his forearm. He had several abrasions, it was bleeding, and dammit it *hurt*. Looking up at David, the tour guide looked as if he'd seen a ghost. "What the hell was *that*?"

That voice came back. "I said, get *out*, goddammit! I'm sick and goddamn tired of goddamn *cat-lovers*!"

Now Greg was starting to get seriously freaked

out. "What— Who—?" *It has to be a recording of some kind, or over a speaker. Has to be.*

Even as he tried to rationalize that, he didn't really believe it. When a voice came over a speaker, you didn't feel the voice in your soul.

The voice continued. "She can stay. *He* has to go!"

"Er," David said, "ah, okay. I mean, of course, Mr. Hemingway."

Greg blinked. "Mr. *Hemingway?*" Now he knew this was some kind of trick. He got unsteadily to his feet, only able to use his left arm and Krysta for support. "This is bogus. Hemingway's *dead*, you stupid dork, and I've got a skinned arm, and I—"

Again with the voice: "Of course I'm *dead*, you numbskull! But this is *my* house, not a cat haven."

Krysta started talking to this thing as if it *was* Hemingway. "I thought you loved cats."

"I loved *my* cat," the voice said. "That doesn't mean I want my house to turn into a goddamned petting zoo! Now get out!"

Greg felt the hands once again, two of them this time, on his chest, even though he couldn't see anyone other than a shocked-looking Krysta and a stone-scared David. He tried to grab at whoever it was, but he just flailed at nothing. The hands pushed him violently backward. Greg tried to keep from backing out through the gate, but the invisible hands were just too strong.

He cried out as he again fell to the ground on his right arm. "Ow! Dammit!"

Krysta ran through the gate after him. As soon as she cleared it, the gate closed with a resounding metallic clang that sent several ivy leaves plummeting to the sidewalk.

"God, Greg, I'm so sorry. I'll call 911." She grabbed her purse and started rummaging around in it for her cell phone.

Greg put his left hand on Krysta's arm. "No, no, it's okay. We'll just go to a drugstore and get something to put on it."

"You sure?"

"The last thing I want to do is try to explain what just happened to an ER nurse."

Krysta smiled. "Okay. C'mon, I think there was a drugstore on Duval."

She helped Greg to his feet. He looked at the Hemingway Home and Museum. He noticed that the young woman in the ticket booth did not consider the manifestation of Hemingway's ghost to be sufficient reason to stop reading about movie stars, as her nose stayed buried in the magazine. "What the hell *was* that?"

"I don't think I wanna know," Krysta said emphatically. "But you were right, coming here was a bad idea."

Greg shook his head as they started walking down Olivia Street toward Duval. "Wow."

"What?"

"That's twice this trip you've admitted I was right."

Primly, Krysta said, "I admit you're right once a year. When I said you were right about Key West being a good vacation spot, it was still 2007. This was the one time I admitted it for '08."

"Whatever you say, my love."

SIX

It was rare that Dean Winchester found himself at a loss for words.

"Um—okay," was all he was able to manage at the revelation that the spirit of Captain Terrence Naylor was standing in front of him and trying to hold a conversation with him. "This is weird."

"You have not answered my question yet!"

Finally, Dean leaned back, angling his body toward the door but not willing to take his eyes off Naylor. "Sam!"

A minute later, he heard Sam's size twelves clomping down the wooden stairs, and his brother came in. "What is it, Dean, I— Oh. It's a spirit."

"Thank you, Captain Obvious," Dean muttered.

Naylor was now folding his ectoplasmic arms over his insubstantial chest. "If one of you would *kindly* explain yourselves."

Sam slowly tore his eyes away from Naylor to look at Dean. "It's a spirit that talks."

"Apparently."

Naylor bellowed, "Stop speaking of me as if I wasn't right here in front of you!"

"Well," Sam said slowly, "you aren't—exactly. You see—you're dead."

"Yes, I'm *aware* of that, if you please," Naylor said testily. "I quite distinctly recall the feeling of the sea overtaking me, the salt water filling my mouth and nose. It was rather unpleasant, and I'm not like to forget it."

Dean frowned. "So you know you're a spirit—a ghost."

"Of *course* I do! And you *still* have not answered—"

"This is a hotel," Sam said. "An inn."

Recalling the history of the place that Bodge had given him when he was here last, Dean added, "Your descendants lived here for a while, then about thirty years ago, some guy tried to turn it into a museum. That tanked pretty bad, and an old woman bought it and turned it into an inn. When she retired, she sold it to a nice young couple, who still run it." Dean figured mentioning that both members of the couple were female wouldn't be such a hot idea.

Scowling, Naylor said, "That's absurd. Why would anyone lodge in my *house*?"

"It's been renovated a bit," Sam said lamely.

"Well, at least you're not screaming," Naylor said, shaking his head.

"What do you mean?" Sam asked. "You've manifested before?"

"I beg your pardon?"

Dean quickly said, "You've talked to other people before us?"

"Of course! Well, not precisely *talked*. I attempted to do so, but they never displayed any form of comprehension. It was most irritating, especially the ear-piercing wails of the girls."

"And you've always been here?" Sam asked.

"Following my death, my soul came to this place. I used to mock those absurd spiritualists that my Agnes would go to. I didn't believe that one could speak to the souls in heaven or in hell. It never occurred to me that they might not actually arrive at either destination. Instead, after death, I found myself here."

"That's not uncommon," Sam said. "Spirits often are drawn after death to places that were important to them in life."

"There has never been anything more important to me than this house, young man, not even the boats I served upon. I was a wrecker for my entire adult life, and I built this house myself. The material was paid for with the wages I earned on the wreckers, and I constructed it with these two good hands." He held out hands that had probably been meaty and calloused when they had had substance.

Dean was about to say something, but the captain kept talking. The poor bastard hadn't had a proper conversation in a hundred fifty years or so, so Dean let him ramble on.

"Eventually, I owned my own vessel and took a wife. Agnes bore me sons and daughters, and I retired so I could watch my children grow. Then she—she passed on from the consumption, and I purchased another boat." He shook his head. "The business had changed, sadly, especially after the War of Northern Aggression ended so poorly."

Somehow, Dean managed not to snort. He knew plenty of modern Southerners who *still* referred to the American Civil War that way.

"Young wreckers who didn't know the reefs and had to be salvaged themselves when they went out. Much more corruption, honorable judges retiring and being replaced by foolish young men who understood nothing of tradition. And then that blessed storm . . ."

Sam looked as though he hadn't followed any of that. Dean only knew what Naylor was talking about by virtue of having visited Key West before. He held up a finger. "Uh, Captain? Look, my brother and I need to, ah, have a conversation in private, okay? We'll be right outside."

"Truly this is a lodging house?"

Nodding, Sam said, "Truly. Um—what year do you think it is, Captain?"

"Well, I perished in the year of our Lord eighteen hundred and seventy-one. I suppose we're approaching the turn of the century now?"

"Actually, we've passed it," Sam said.

"Twice," Dean added helpfully. "It's now *twenty* hundred and eight."

Naylor's face fell. "It's been *that* long?"

"'Fraid so." Dean grabbed Sam's shoulder and hustled him out through the porch door. "Now then, if you'll excuse us."

They went out, Dean slid the door shut, and they walked out into the garden. "It's that Molly chick and Farmer Greeley all over again," he said.

Sam shook his head. "Yeah, but this is a lot different. Molly and Greeley only manifested once a year. That's why they were solid and speaking, it was a whole year's worth of spiritual energy concentrated into a single day. Plus, they were tied to a particular time and place. But going from a typical haunting to something like this—that's new." Sam scratched the back of his head. "What was all that about wrecking things?"

Dean was unable to help smiling at the opportunity to lecture Sam for a change. "He was a wrecker—it was the big business around here in the nineteenth century."

"They'd deliberately wreck ships? That's awful."

"No, dumb-ass, the ships'd get wrecked all by themselves. There's reefs out there up the ass, and ships would get nailed all the time. Remember, most boats were wood back then. The wreckers were salvage ships that would rescue the boats."

Looking back at the bungalow, Sam said, "So he was a pirate."

"That's what I thought, too, at first," Dean said with a chuckle. "But no, it was all legit. Was pretty heavily regulated, too, but people who were good at it made a bundle. Half the nice houses on the island were built by wreckers and their families."

"Huh." Sam put his hands on his hips. "So now what?"

Dean shrugged. "Now nothin'. Yaphet said the spirits on the island were more active. This proves it wasn't just him bein' stoned."

"This is more than just active, Dean, this is—I don't now, supercharged."

"Yeah," Dean said, "that'd take some serious mojo."

Sighing, Sam said, "Which makes it even more likely that it's one of our Wyoming refugees." He pulled his Treo out of his pants pocket. "I'm gonna give Bobby a call."

"Okay. I'm gonna see what I can do about my roommate situation."

As Sam put the phone to his ear, Dean stepped

back up onto the porch and slid the door open. "Captain?"

"Have you and your sibling conferred?" he asked snidely.

"Look—can you haunt one of the other bungalows? I mean, Sammy and I—we'd like our privacy, y'know?"

"I might be willing to accede to your request, young man, assuming you can explain to me why you have responded to me so differently from everyone else."

"Couple reasons," Dean said. "One, my brother Sam and I, we're hunters. We fight demons and vampires and the like."

"This is a common practice in this century, is it?"

"Uh, no, actually—we're kind of under the radar."

"Under the what?"

Recalling that radar wasn't developed until the twentieth century, Dean amended his statement. "We're a secret society."

Naylor rolled his eyes. "Like the thrice-damned Freemasons, I suppose."

"Uh, sort of." Dean figured that was as good an analogy as any, though he would've killed for the Freemasons' resources.

"You said a 'couple' of reasons. What is the other?"

"Normally, spirits like you aren't able to contact living people so—so precisely. I've been doing this most of my life, and I usually can't have a conversation with a spirit like this. Which means there's someone or something on this island that's messing around with the dead."

"And you intend to take arms against this someone or something?"

"That's the plan, yeah."

Again, Naylor folded his arms. "And what becomes of me should you be successful?"

Dean let out a breath. "You go back to what you were before. Or—" He hesitated. "Or we salt and burn your remains, and you move on to whatever afterlife you're supposed to go to."

"Then I will enter into this agreement with you, young man."

Fed up with feeling like he was in the principal's office, he said, "My name's Dean. Dean Winchester. Not 'young man.'"

For the first time, Naylor smiled. "Very well, Mr. Winchester—the terms of the agreement are thus: I will not disturb your privacy for the duration of your stay in my house. In return, I request that, should you and your brother be successful in your endeavors, that you retrieve my remains from under the walnut tree in the garden, salt and burn them as you say, and free my soul from this wretched place."

Unable to help himself, Dean said cheekily, "I thought this was the most important place in your life."

"It was. But my life is over, and this is no longer my home. It is past time I moved on, don't you think, Mr. Winchester?"

Since that plan had been in the back of Dean's mind in any case—leaving aside any other considerations, the spirit would be bad for Nicki and Bodge's business—it was easy enough for him to say, "Sure, no problem."

"Normally at this juncture, I would spit on my hand and offer it to you."

"Let's not and say we did," Dean said, as Sam slid the door open with one hand while placing his phone back in his pocket with the other. "What'd Bobby say?"

Sam cut his eyes toward Naylor, but Dean waved him off. "He's cool."

After giving Dean a we'll-talk-about-this-later look, Sam said, "Bobby hasn't heard of anything like this, either, but he said he'd dig through his library and see what turns up."

Dean liked it better when Bobby knew everything off the top of his head, which meant Dean could cut right to the part where they kicked ass.

Sam continued: "He also said that this is the first time Yaphet's been right about anything since he said the Beatles would break up."

That got a laugh from Dean. "C'mon, let's check across the street, then track down Yaphet."

"Best of luck, gentlemen," Naylor said. "May God be with you—for all our sakes."

Then the spirit disappeared. No fading, no movement—one second he was there, the next he wasn't.

Dean looked at Sam and grinned. "Spooky."

To his credit, Sam didn't dignify that awful joke with a reply. "Why's he wishing us luck?"

As they left, Dean explained his conversation with the captain. He finished with: "It's weird."

"What do you mean?"

"Well, we salt and burn these people 'cause they're causing a fuss. Never really thought about it from the spirit's side. Remember that job in New York we did about a year or so back?"

Sam smiled as they went into the main house through the back door. "I remember you geeking out over the guy's vinyl collection."

Ignoring the dig—although Manfred Afiri did have an *amazing* record collection that Dean seriously envied—he said, "We didn't salt and burn the bones because we needed the body to prove that she'd been killed."

"I remember, yeah. You think we should've?"

After giving a quick wave to Bodge, sitting at the front desk, they went out the front door. "I dunno. I mean, Manfred has both our numbers, and he

woulda called if the spirit acted up again, but—"
He shook his head as he swung the wrought-iron
gate open with a low squeak. "Did we do her spirit
any favors by not letting her move on?"

Sam peered down at his brother. "Since when
are *you* the whiny emo bitch of this partnership?"

Rolling his eyes, Dean said, "Kiss my ass,
Sammy, you know what I mean."

"I do, I'm just stunned to hear *you* say it."

"What, I can't be philosophical once in a
while?"

Sam smiled. "As long as it's only once in a while,
I guess."

"Gee thanks."

They crossed Eaton and approached the house
with the turret.

Unfortunately, the door was locked, crime-scene
tape flapped in one of the bushes in front of the
house, and the sign in the window read CLOSED
UNTIL FURTHER NOTICE.

"Guess a double homicide really *is* bad for business," Sam muttered.

"Yeah. I'd rather wait until there's a few fewer
folks on the street before we try going at it with
our mad lockpicking skillz."

Sam gave Dean a withering look. "Right. So
what, we talk to this Yaphet guy?"

"May as well." Dean chuckled. "Remember how
Manfred was a trip back to the sixties?"

"Yeah."

"Yaphet's worse."

Shuddering, Sam said, "Okay, now I'm scared."

At that, Dean just grinned as he led Sam toward Duval Street.

Ah, this is the life, Dean thought as he felt the cool breeze blow through his short hair, the very un-January-like warmth, and the sounds of music blaring from all around. Just by moving the half block to Duval Street, it was like they entered a whole different place. Eaton Street was quiet and mostly residential. Duval was commercial, with stores, restaurants, and bars—and people. Both the sidewalks and the streets were filled with pedestrians, some traveling in drunken groups. Cars inched down the road, making appallingly slow progress. Dean could hear half a dozen bass lines vying for his attention, not to mention the occasional wail of someone crooning along to a karaoke machine.

"*God*, I missed this place," Dean said, looking over at Sam.

"Why am I not surprised?" Sam said with mild distaste.

Dean shook his head. "College was wasted on you, dude."

They walked across Duval and at the corner of Caroline Street came upon the Bull—which was the downstairs part. Upstairs was the Whistle, which had a pool table and a jukebox and people out on the balcony. The Bull was downstairs and had a small stage where music acts played. Like most of the places on Duval, the Bull was open-air, with huge windows open on both the Duval side and the Caroline side. Through those windows, Dean could see two guys with acoustic guitars playing, and the tables full of people sipping drinks. As they got closer, he could make out the strains of The Who's "Pinball Wizard" from the two guys on the stage.

Much as he wanted to go in and listen to them for a while, they had business, especially since, as promised, their quarry was sitting on the Caroline Street sidewalk. Dean had been hoping he wouldn't be there, so they'd have an excuse to walk farther down Duval to the Hog's Breath, passing even more bars on the way. But it was not to be.

Yaphet the Poet looked exactly the same as he did four years earlier: long gray hair that started with a sharp widow's peak at his forehead and hung loosely around his shoulders at the other end; a thick gray beard that went down to his chest; round glasses with no lenses that he still wore even though they did nothing to correct his vision; rheumy brown eyes; a tie-dyed shirt that had several holes and looked like it hadn't been laundered since the last time Dean saw him; cutoff denim shorts that covered bony, hairy legs; and bare feet that were covered in calluses and sores.

He was seated on the sidewalk, back up against the wall of the Bull. Next to him, also leaning against the wall, was a large piece of battered corkboard. Brightly colored pushpins kept several sheets of paper attached to it, each of which contained a poem written in flowery-yet-legible handwriting, as well as a sign on top that said YAPHET'S POEMS, $1 EACH. In front of the corkboard was a small bowl with flowers painted on it, and several dollar bills and coins inside it.

At the brothers' approach, Yaphet's head tilted up. "Dean! Wow, man, it really is you!"

"Toldja we'd be down, Yaphet. This is my brother, Sam."

"Totally groovy to meet you, Sam."

"Uh, likewise."

Dean chuckled. "So, we've already seen our first ghost."

"Wow, and you, like, just got here, man. That's cool. Who was it?"

Quickly, Dean filled Yaphet in on their encounter with Captain Naylor.

"Far out, man. Lookie, there's more than just those three people who croaked. We got us a celebrity spook, too. Papa's at the Hemingway pad."

Sam's eyes went wide. "*Ernest* Hemingway?"

"Right on, brother. Papa, he went and scared off all the kitty-cats, and some'a the *turistas*, too. Nobody croaked yet, but a whole lotta bruisin'."

Dean looked at Sam. "We'll have to check it out."

"Easy enough," Yaphet said. "Papa's pad is still open for business."

"You're kidding," Sam said. "Even after people were injured?"

Yaphet shrugged. "Don't look at me, man, I just live here."

Sam said, "We should go there right now, then, before somebody else gets hurt."

"Yeah." Dean looked back at Yaphet. "What about the girl whose throat was cut?"

"I saw her, actually. She didn't buy no poems or nothin', but least she was polite about it. Went into the Hog's Breath. Didn't see her leave, though— prolly went out the back, since they found her on Front. Sulfur in the wound, too, so you know what *that's* all about. Ain't heard nothin' beyond that, except the spooks went into overdrive after she kicked the bucket."

Sam blew out a breath through his teeth. "That fits. Like you said, Dean, major mojo, and if a human sacrifice was involved, that'd make the spell powerful enough to do what this one's done."

"Waitasec," Dean said, remembering something, "I thought you said the spooks kicked it up a notch six months ago."

"They did, man—it was just normal hauntin', though, like usual, just lots and lots more of it.

After that girl got dead, it went up *another* notch. Totally uncool, man."

"So they're escalating," Sam said. "Hate to think what stage three is."

Dean nodded. "C'mon, let's lock and load, then pay a visit to a dead writer." Reaching into his pocket, Dean pulled out a ten-dollar bill and dropped it into the bowl.

"Hey, thanks, man! That means you get yourself ten poems!"

"I'll pass, thanks," Dean said.

Sam, though, peered down at the corkboard. "I'll take one, if that's okay."

Dean rolled his eyes. "You are *such* a geek."

Yaphet, though, said, "Absitively, man. Pick any one you want."

After glancing up and down the board, Sam looked down at Yaphet. "Which one do you recommend?"

Leaning to his left, Yaphet pulled out a red pushpin and removed the poem that was on the top left. "This one's called 'Ode to Bong Water.' I think it truly speaks to the hearts and minds of everyone, you know what I'm sayin'?"

Dean had to hold in a guffaw at the look of distaste on Sam's face. "Uh, no, that doesn't sound like it's for me." He looked at the corkboard again and pointed at the one in the center. "How about this one?"

"That's my latest—'Sonnet for a Sunset.' Play on words, man, you dig?"

Smiling, Sam took that one off the corkboard and gave Yaphet a dollar.

"Hey, man, you don't gotta do that. Your brother covered you."

"It's okay—an artist deserves to be paid for his work."

Rubbing his forehead with a combination of amusement and pity, Dean said, "Catch you later, Yaphet. We're at the Naylor House, so if you hear anything, let Nicki or Bodge know."

"Groovy, man. Keep on truckin', you hear?"

Grinning, Sam said, "Absitively."

SEVEN

Jorge smiled at the look of glee on his brother Reynaldo's face as they approached the Little White House.

Reynaldo had always hated the tropics. He joked that he had to have his tolerance for humidity removed when he moved from Puerto Rico to New York. As a result, it was damn near impossible for Jorge to get Reynaldo to visit him and his boyfriend Silas on Key West. They'd gone up to New York several times for Christmas—Silas, a native Floridian, had never seen snow in his life until their first visit—but Jorge kept making excuses for not coming down.

That changed when Reynaldo's son, Pablo—who, everyone agreed, was the only good thing to come out of his marriage—started learning about the presidents of the United States in school. With the obsessiveness that only an eight-year-old could have, Pablo became the world's biggest president geek, wanting to know everything about all of them—how they were elected, what they did while in office, and so on. Reynaldo had had to read a ton of material in order to keep up with Pablo's questions.

But while Pablo's obsession burned out fairly quickly as he moved on to other things, Reynaldo kept up with the reading, and became an even bigger geek than his offspring.

That, in turn, finally got him to visit Key West. Reynaldo had said he'd tolerate the tropical heat and humidity only if Jorge and Silas promised to take him to the Little White House. He waited until after the New Year because he got a cheaper flight (Reynaldo had child-support payments and a low-paying civil-service job; he had to cut corners where he could).

So now they were standing at the entrance on Front Street, and Reynaldo looked like the Rapture had come and Jesus just told him his room in heaven was all reserved.

They paid their admission and joined the rest of the tour group—which was pretty small, all things considered. Just the three of them, plus a woman and a little boy with her coloring, so probably a mother and child. Their guide was a perky young blonde named Laurie, who gave the history of the building in a high-pitched, squeaky drawl.

"Originally the Little White House was built for the U.S. Navy. The naval base here was a *very* important part of the United States' defense against sea attack from our enemies. What is *now* the Little White House was quarters for *important* people who served the base. By the turn of the century, it was converted into a single-family dwelling for the base *commandant*."

The woman raised the hand that wasn't holding that of her son and spoke in a small voice, thick with an accent that sounded Russian. "Excuse me—did not Thomas Edison live here?"

"Yes, he did!" Laurie practically squealed, as if the woman was a first grader who'd gotten a tough question right. "During the *First* World War, Thomas Edison—the father of modern electricity—lived here while helping the U.S. Navy in their effort against the *evil* Axis powers."

Jorge rolled his eyes at Silas. Reynaldo, though, had to say something, as usual. "Uh, excuse me, ma'am, but we fought the Axis powers in World War *Two*."

Laurie just stared at Reynaldo for a second, then moved on. "President Harry S Truman *first* visited here in 1946, looking for a place for rest and relaxation. For President Truman, the buck *didn't* stop at Camp David." Laurie smiled at her half witticism, which was more than Jorge was able to manage.

Reynaldo, though, had to comment again. "It wasn't called Camp David back then, it was called Shangri-La. That's what FDR named it. Eisenhower renamed it Camp David after his grandson."

Silas whispered in his ear, "Your brother came down just to get pissed off?"

Jorge just shrugged. Silas grabbed his hand and gave it a sympathetic squeeze.

Laurie, having decided just to ignore Reynaldo, led them through various rooms, giving the history of the place. Truman apparently signed some bills and worked on State of the Union addresses here, among other things. "In addition, after President Truman left office, *other* presidents used this site, from President *Eisenhower,* who came here to recover from a heart attack, to President *Kennedy,* who came here after the Cuban *Missile* Crisis, to President *Carter,* who held a family reunion here. It's still available for any president to use, and in fact Secretary of State Colin *Powell* held peace talks here between the presidents of Armenia and Uzbekistan."

Reynaldo winced. "That was Azerbaijan," he said in a tight voice.

Again, Laurie stared, then led them through another room. This was a huge space with plenty of chairs, a large window that overlooked the sea, and a big table in the center. As she walked in backward, Laurie was droning on. "President Truman *loved* to play poker, and he had a table in this room that he used for games. But he had to be *careful*, because of course the president couldn't be seen to be *gambling*, so there was a cover for the table for when *reporters* came by."

Jorge, though, wasn't really listening to what Laurie was saying, and only partly because she was vapid and annoying. Instead, he was staring at the poker table and felt his jaw drop open.

Laurie actually noticed this, and her pert face scrunched into a frown. "What are you all staring at?"

The young boy answered. "There's a man there!"

Turning around, Laurie saw what Jorge saw: an old white man with short gray hair, large round glasses, and a bright smile. He was wearing a straw hat, a white button-down shirt, and white pants, and he was shuffling a deck of cards.

Reynaldo's Rapture look came back. "Holy Mary, Mother of God, that's Harry Truman!"

"It—it *can't* be!" Laurie looked as if her brain had short-circuited, a feeling Jorge could sympathize with. "Isn't he, like, *dead*?"

Truman set the cards down and his smile got wider. "Well? Someone gonna cut the deck? It's five-card draw, jacks or better to open, trips or better to win."

Jorge was starting to think that maybe this trip was worth it for Reynaldo after all . . .

EIGHT

David Madleigh had never been so scared in his life.

Admittedly, the competition wasn't exactly what you'd call fierce. David was pushing thirty and still hadn't figured out what to do with his life. He had two bachelor's degrees and a master's. When he completed the latter, he came down to Key West to take a summer off and just hang out, go to the beach, drink a lot of beer, listen to a lot of music, do some snorkeling, maybe learn how to scuba dive, and so on, before moving back north to work on his Ph.D.

That was five years ago. He hadn't gotten around to leaving the island yet.

The money he'd saved up for the vacation had run out, so he had to work, and since his MA was in English literature anyhow, what better use to put it to than to work at the Hemingway Home and Museum?

That was fine right up until Hemingway's ghost showed up.

David had heard all the ghost stories. Hell, he'd even done a few ghost tours on a freelance basis over the past five years. But he'd never actually seen a ghost—until six months ago.

It had actually been kind of cool at first. The ghost didn't really *do* anything except glare a lot, but that pretty much fit Hemingway's intense personality. This was a guy who fought bulls, after all.

Then he started talking.

And acting.

The historical society insisted on keeping the place open. Business was bad enough in January once the holiday crowd disappeared, they didn't want to make it worse. David's argument that they weren't going to get a lot of people anyhow fell on deaf ears. He had to keep giving tours and hoping that nobody would mention the cats—like that poor guy this morning.

And sure enough, the place was deserted this evening. Nobody had shown up for the 6:15 tour, and he was willing to bet that the same would be true for the 7:15.

Then two guys came in—one very tall, one just the regular kind of tall, both going for a sort of post-Grunge look. They were also a little ripe, like their last shower was in 2007. The taller one was carrying a packing tube of some kind. The shorter one was holding what looked like an old Sony Walkman that had been attacked by a rabid dog, and also wore a necklace with some kind of weird charm. The taller one approached David after the two paid their way.

"Hi there. I'm Sam Winchester, this is my brother, Dean."

David smiled. He'd pegged them for a couple, not siblings. "My name's David, and I'll be running the tour, which starts at fifteen minutes past the hour. Until then, I'll be happy to answer any questions you might have. The house was orig—"

Sam interrupted him. "We're actually curious about the hauntings."

Sweat, which the mild breeze did nothing to ameliorate, beaded on David's forehead. "You talked to that couple, didn't you?"

"I'm sorry?" Sam put on a confused expression, but David wasn't buying it.

"Look, that man just tripped and fell on the sidewalk. There are a lot of cracks—Katrina, y'know? Messed up all the sidewalks around here." In fact, most of the sidewalks had been fixed up in the two and a half years since Hurricane Katrina, but David had to say *something* . . .

"I don't know what man you're talking about," Sam said. "We just—"

A noise startled David, causing him to jump up a few inches in the air and his heart to skip a beat. Whirling around, he saw Sam's brother, Dean, raising his arms and dropping his messed-up Walkman. Looking down on the pavement, David saw that the Walkman was sparking, lights flashing on and off.

Sam looked at Dean. "Dude—the EMF blew out."

"You think?" Dean said, shaking his hand back and forth. "Christ, the energy you'd need for that'd light up Chicago. Definitely some major mojo here."

David had no idea what these two were talking about, but he needed to get them out of here before Mr. Hemingway showed up. "All right, look, I don't know what you two are doing, but—"

Turning back to David, Sam said, "We need to know about the haunting. When did it start?"

"I—I don't know what—"

Walking up to him, Sam stared down at him with scary-intense eyes. "Look, David, something bad's happening here. We need to stop it. People have been hurt and killed."

The sweat was now pouring down into David's eyes. He removed his glasses and wiped his eyes with the sleeve of his T-shirt. "K-killed? I don't know what you're—"

"When did the hauntings start?"

"About—about six months ago. Mr. Hemingway just kept—kept *appearing*, y'know? And it was cool and all, but then—but then he started *talking* to people." He looked away. "Then he got rid of the cats."

Sam frowned. "Cats."

"Yeah, I was wonderin' about that," Dean said. "The museum's famous for having lots of cats. They all got six toes, supposedly."

"Right," Sam said with a nod, "because Hemingway had polydactyl cats."

David ignored the glare that Dean gave Sam at that comment, and said, "And he kept checking on the tourists. Mostly it was okay, but if anyone was here to see the cats instead of his home, he'd throw them out!" It was actually kind of a relief to *talk* about this. The staff had been dancing around the issue, kind of pretending nothing untoward was happening.

"When did he become so active?" Sam asked.

"Last week. Couple days before New Year's."

Sam looked at Dean. "When that girl died."

David frowned. "What girl?"

"Never mind," Sam said. "Do you know when he'll show up again?"

"That's easy," Dean said with a smirk before David could say that he had no idea. Talking a lot louder, Dean said, "Well, shoot, Sammy, if the cats aren't here, we may as well go home! Nobody cares about some musty old writer dude, we just wanna see the cool cats!"

Closing his eyes, David said, "You'll hear him now."

Sam asked, "Hear? Not see?"

David reopened his eyes to see a look of confusion on Sam's features. "Yeah, when he throws people out, you can't see him. If he just wants to yell at you—and he does that a lot, lemme tell ya—then you can see him."

"Good," Dean said. "Means they have limits."

An all-too-damn-familiar voice said, "Limits are for the living, boy."

Both brothers looked around, but couldn't see anything. Dean looked at his brother. "Sam!"

But Sam was already reaching into the tube he was carrying, and pulled out two sawed-off shotguns. He tossed one to Dean, who caught it one-handed.

Panic suffused David. The only guns that were supposed to be there were from Mr. Hemingway's collection.

Dean started waving the shotgun around. "Where are you, you dead bastard?"

"Impressive," Mr. Hemingway's voice said. Suddenly, the air shifted and the form of Mr. Hemingway coalesced right in front of Dean. "You do those modifications yourself, boy?"

That threw Dean for a loop, apparently, as his mouth fell open. "Uh, yeah—yeah, I did."

Sam, meanwhile, took aim with his shotgun and fired it, the report reverberating in David's ears.

David's father used to hunt all the time, and taught David all kinds of things he didn't care about regarding firearms. Since leaving home, David had willfully forgotten most of what his father had taught him, but he remembered just enough to know that shotgun blasts usually didn't look like that. It was a spray of what looked like sand or dirt or salt or something.

Whatever it was, it had an immediate effect on Mr. Hemingway, who looked like he literally blew apart, his screams echoing off the house and competing with the shotgun blast to completely deafen David.

Over the ringing in his ears that made everything echo like they were in a tunnel, David heard Dean say, "Y'know, this whole conversational thing is really messing with my game. Was he really geeking out over my sawed-off?"

Ever the tour guide, David found himself saying, "Mr. Hemingway was a connoisseur of firearms in his life." He said it in a high, squeaky voice, and not entirely consciously. His ears were *still* ringing, and his feet were rooted to the spot. He didn't think he could move if someone put a gun to his head—which was a real possibility just now.

"That . . . hurt!"

All three of them looked around. That was Mr. Hemingway's voice.

Sam had once again raised his shotgun. "*Definitely* some major mojo."

"*Oh* yeah," Dean said, doing likewise.

"Hey," David said, "you really can't have those in here!"

"Rock salt disperses spirits," Sam said.

That brought David up short. "Really?"

"Yup. These shotguns fire rock-salt rounds. It won't hurt anything."

David probably should have pointed out that even rock salt can cause damage to physical objects if thrust with great force out of a shotgun barrel, but a voice sounded in the courtyard.

"You . . . *shot* . . . me!"

The voice was still disembodied, which worried David, as it probably meant he was going to do something physical.

"Yeah, well, it's what we do," Dean said. "Call it revenge for all the kids who had to suffer through *The Old Man and the Sea* in school."

"Shoot . . . a man . . . in his . . . *home*?"

"No, shoot a spirit who's infesting a museum," Dean said. "C'mon, 'Papa,' show yourself. Face me like a man!"

Having already reached what he'd thought was his panic threshold, David found himself panicking *more*. Appealing to Mr. Hemingway's *machismo* was a *bad* idea.

"Oh . . . I will, boy . . . rest assured. Very . . . very . . . soon." Those last three words were a bit quieter, as if a song was fading out at the end.

"I think we got him," Sam said. "Just took a little longer."

"Yeah," Dean said, "and I get the feeling he's gonna pull himself together faster'n usual, too." He looked at David. "We need to salt and burn his bones. Where's he buried?"

David's mind went blank for a second, then he stammered, "Er, uh—Idaho."

"Crap." Dean shook his head.

Sam approached David. Where before he was intense, now he was pleading. "Listen, David, we're staying at the Naylor House—you know the place?"

Quickly, nervously, David nodded.

"If the spirit comes back, call there and let one of the proprietors know, okay?"

"O-okay."

"Freeze!"

Whirling around, David saw Officer Van Montrose standing in the entryway, his weapon out and pointed at Sam and Dean.

"Drop the shotguns and put your hands behind your heads, fellas," Montrose said in his deep voice.

"Officer—" Sam started, but Montrose cut him off.

"I didn't say talk, I said drop the shotguns and put your hands behind your heads—*now!*"

Sam and Dean did as they were told. "On your knees, interlock your fingers," Montrose added. As they did so—Sam looking resigned, Dean looking pissed—Montrose said, "Heard a shotgun blast, David. What happened?"

"These two guys were firing—firing rock salt at—at, you know, the—the thing." Even with the frank talk with Sam and Dean, David couldn't bring himself to say "Mr. Hemingway's ghost" out loud.

"Rock salt?" Montrose asked. "You sure?"

David nodded quickly.

"Okay." Montrose walked around behind Sam and grabbed one arm, bringing it down to the small of his back, and attached a handcuff to that wrist, then did the same for the other arm. He then cuffed Dean, and yanked both to their feet. "C'mon, fellas, we're goin' for a ride."

David swallowed. The ringing in his ears was finally starting to die down, so the world was starting to sound normal again.

"You okay, David?" Montrose asked.

"Not really. You, uh—you need me to make a statement?"

"If I do, I'll come by later, all right?"

David nodded as Montrose led the brothers out of the courtyard and to the street.

It was several minutes before he moved from that spot.

Dean was fairly used to being handcuffed.

Between his various arrests and some of his kinkier one-nighters, Dean had worn the bracelets many a time. He'd learned the hard way that struggling was pointless and only served to make it hurt more, as the thin metal bit into your wrists. Dean didn't mind pain, and had a fairly high tolerance for it, but that didn't mean he sought it out, either. So when he was cuffed in the courtyard of the Hemingway Home and Museum, he didn't struggle or complain.

Sam hadn't been handcuffed nearly as often—he had neither been arrested enough nor had an interesting enough sex life—so he hadn't figured that out yet. He was still struggling as the cop hustled them to his cruiser, parked at an angle in front of the Hemingway Home and Museum.

This was a complication they didn't need. There were federal warrants out on both Dean and Sam, and an FBI agent named Victor Henriksen who was just dying to get his mitts on them again. Dean really couldn't blame Henriksen—he was just doing his job, and from the point of view of a federal agent who didn't know the real deal, Dean was a crazed serial killer and Sam his accomplice. But Dean would also be quite happy never to see the man ever again, either. Henriksen had learned from the mistakes he'd made in Milwaukee and adjusted his game plan accordingly when he encountered them again in Green River. The next time, he'd likely learn from the brand-new mistakes at Green River and make their lives even *more* difficult.

Which meant they had to get away from the Key West cops. Or at least this cop. He had a flat face, a big nose, and small eyes, with jet-black hair. He pronounced his vowels in that funny way that was common to a lot of Native Americans, so Dean figured he was Seminole or some such. Dean was encouraged by the fact that the cop couldn't even be bothered to frisk Sam and Dean before putting them in the car, thus missing the burned-out EMF in Dean's pocket. It meant a level of incompetence that might make escape very possible.

After putting them in the backseat and their shotguns in the passenger seat next to him, the cop climbed into the front. He checked both shotguns, laughed, shook his head, started the ignition— Dean heard the engine pull a bit and thought it needed a tune-up, not that he intended to share that with the cop—and backed up a bit before heading down Whitehall.

"Where you two staying?" the cop asked.

"Sorry," Dean said, "I'm invoking my right to remain silent."

The cop shrugged. "Fine, I'll just drop you off wherever."

Dean frowned. "What?"

"You fellas're walkin' around with rock-salt rounds in your shotguns. Means you're either nuts, in which case the paperwork'll be a pain in the ass, or you're hunters."

Sam and Dean exchanged confused and surprised glances. This was unexpected. "Uh, well—"

"I got standing orders to let hunters be. You fellas come through here a lot, after all."

"Uh, yeah," Dean said. "We're hunters. There's been a lot of—"

"Yeah, I know, the spooks're on overload. Figured one or two'a you guys'd be along soon enough. They shut down the Little White House today, too, after a tour group saw Harry S his *own* self playin' poker."

For a brief moment, Dean thought how cool it would be to play poker with the ghost of Harry Truman, then quickly banished the thought.

"We'll need to check that out," Sam said.

"I wouldn't," the cop said, turning the car onto Virginia Street. "Keep in mind, presidents and other big-shot folk *still* come there occasionally, and the Secret Service has been known to appear. When they lock down, they lock *down*."

Sam nodded. "We'll bear that in mind—and, uh, we're staying at the Naylor House."

Dean could see the cop smile in the rearview mirror. "Good place. Give Nicki and Bodge my regards." He turned up Duval Street, and they moved agonizingly slowly up the street. It was packed with people barhopping, and even the fact that they were in a police car couldn't make the backlog of cars move any faster.

"Uh, these standing orders," Sam said slowly. "*All* the local cops have them?"

That got another smile. "Some of us, yeah. The ones who know what's really goin' on."

"You wouldn't happen to know a cop in New York named McBain, would you?" Sam asked. "Or one in Baltimore named Ballard?"

"Nah. Why?"

"No reason."

Dean chuckled at his brother's question. A cop in NYPD's Missing Persons Unit was part of what she called a network of police who knew about the supernatural. Said "network" consisted of only three or four others—including Ballard, a homicide cop Sam and Dean had encountered in Baltimore. Sam was probably thinking that this guy should be part of it. For his part, Dean wasn't interested. Mostly his life was easier when he stayed three steps ahead of law enforcement, the vast majority of whom were mentally incapable of dealing with what Dean and Sam dealt with every day. Sam would probably point out that Dean and Sam wouldn't be very good at dealing with, say, homicidal junkies. But cops had their job, and Sam and Dean had theirs. The world was a better place when they just stayed out of each other's way.

Eventually, they made it to Eaton, and the cop turned and parked in front of the tour place across the street. He opened the door and uncuffed them, handing them each their shotguns as well as a business card each.

"My name's Montrose. You need anything, call that number—it's my cell."

Dean had no intention of using it, but Sam said, "Thanks—we appreciate it."

"And hey, take a shower, willya? You two were stinkin' up my radio car."

With that, he got back into his car and drove off.

Walking across the street, Sam said, "Officer Montrose was right. We *are* getting a little ripe."

Since they hadn't showered since they left Bobby's, Dean grudgingly had to concede the point, though he refused to do so out loud. "Fine, let's take care of that, then hit the bars."

"Dean—" Sam started.

"Look, our next step is to check out the place across the street, right? So we do that later on, when the streets are a little emptier."

Sam glanced down at Duval, just a few feet down the street, and saw the teeming mass of drunken humanity stumbling around. "Yeah, good point."

"Besides," Dean added with a grin, "I could use some good tunes."

Predictably, Sam rolled his eyes. Dean sighed, and they went inside the Naylor House.

NINE

Tom Tracy was really hoping to get lucky.

He had taken the construction job in Key West precisely because he knew it had to be a good place to find hot women. After all, they filmed *Girls Gone Wild* videos down here.

It was a simple plan: He intended to sleep with as many young, pretty women as he possibly could, and take photos of the act (or at least of the women, if they couldn't be convinced to have pictures taken of them naked), and send those photos to his ex-girlfriend.

Yeah, it was petty. But Missy said that he wasn't any good in bed anymore, and that was why she broke up with him, and that royally pissed Tom off.

I'll show her just how good I am. Bitch.

So far, though, he hadn't had as much luck as he'd have wanted. The first woman he took back to the small attic apartment he'd rented for the duration of the job threw up as soon as she reached the top of the stairs and insisted on going back to her hotel after that. The second one passed out after taking her clothes off. (He got a picture of her lying naked on the bed, though—he'd tell Missy it was after the act.) The third turned out to be a guy in drag. Tom actually went ahead and took a picture of him, just to mess with Missy's head, but no way in hell he was getting into bed with *that*. (The transvestite actually took it pretty well, and they'd parted on good terms, the guy even recommending a good steakhouse on Cow Key.)

Tonight, he was getting number four if it killed him.

He'd started out at the Whistle, and now had moved on to Rick's. A huge complex that included several dance floors on several levels, there was a DJ playing dance music on one of them. Tom had never been a fan of this kind of music, but he knew that college girls liked it, and he figured if he went to the dance floor and started in with one of them, he might achieve number four—and actually *get* laid this time, dammit!

Besides, the DJ wasn't likely to play "Brown-Eyed Girl." If Tom never heard that goddamn song again, it'd be too soon . . .

The first few young girls he'd tried to dance with had inched away from him as he got closer, but there was this one who seemed to enjoy the attention. Dark-haired (tied back in a ponytail that whipped around with her head movements), big catlike brown eyes, a pointed nose, and *fantastic* cheekbones, she was quite a looker.

She was also really into the music, so much so that Tom wasn't even sure he'd be able to get her attention, but after a minute of moving close to her, she moved closer to *him* and started gyrating toward him—not quite touching, but coming very close, the way strippers did when they did a lap dance.

This girl was good-looking enough to *be* a stripper, in Tom's considered and experienced opinion. She had a classic hourglass figure, with boobs that looked to be at least D cups, flat stomach, decent hips. She wore a loose white tank top over a bikini top that did a very poor job of containing said D cups, which suited Tom just fine, and a pair of denim cutoffs. She had fantastic legs, and a huge smile, which she flashed at Tom as he danced closer to her.

They kept at it for two more songs, getting closer and closer with each passing second. He could smell the tequila on her breath, mixed with the sweat of their exertions. He also noticed that she spent plenty of time staring at his broad chest and well-muscled arms.

After one song ended and as a new one was starting, Tom decided to make his move. Leaning into the side of her head, he shouted into her ear, "Can I buy you a drink?"

Out came the big smile, and she nodded. He grabbed her hand and led her through the hordes of dancers toward the nearest bar. "Jack Daniel's, straight up, and whatever the lady wants."

"The lady wants tequila," she said. Her voice was a bit hoarse. Based on the sweat that glistened on her smooth skin, she'd been here a while, so she'd probably been shouting a lot.

Holding out his hand, he said, "I'm Tom."

"Teresa. You got great moves, Tom."

"So do you," Tom said. "You got great eyes."

She laughed. "They're okay, but my boobs are better. They're all natural, too."

Okay, I was gonna take it slow, but this is fine, too. This also relieved Tom of having to pretend to not be staring at her chest. "Very nice."

The bartender brought the drinks, and Tom paid cash—he didn't want to run up a tab, as he had no intention of staying at the bar that long.

The two of them quickly grew tired of shouting, especially since Teresa's voice was getting scratchier by the second. Tom asked the bartender for a glass of ice water for her, and they moved downstairs to where there were small round tables far enough from the DJs and bands that you could have a civilized conversation. There were some pizza and ice-cream places nearby, and the other folks at the tables had the look of people who needed a break from dancing and/or some food for a pick-me-up.

Tom soon learned that Teresa was an administrative assistant for an accountant in Miami. She was thinking of quitting, though, and becoming a model. "I've even got some pictures up on a few websites. It's good money, and the secretary job is just so *boring*. Plus my boss is a *total* dork."

"You'd make a great model."

She whipped out the smile again. "So would you. You work out?"

"Don't need to—I work construction."

The cat eyes widened to the size of saucers, and her mouth formed an O. "*Really*? Oh, wow."

"Yeah, we're buildin' a new house on a place down on South Street that got wrecked by Katrina. Some rich people bought the lot, demolished what was left of the old place, and my company got brought in to put up a new one. Place is gonna look *great,* too."

"Can you take me to it?"

Tom blinked. "Uh—"

"I just *love* construction sites—they really turn me on. It's like—everything's just pure *potential*. I love trying to imagine what it would become."

She had him at "turn me on." Gulping down the last of his JD, he said, "C'mon, let's go."

At that, she actually squealed. Tom had never heard anyone squeal in real life before.

The site was all the way at the southern end of the island, which was a bit far to walk, so he called for a cab on his cell, then walked with Teresa over to Whitehall—it'd take forever for the cab to get in and out of Duval Street, and Tom had learned early on that just moving one block off the main drag made a huge difference.

Teresa was clinging to him the entire time, and in the cab she was practically sitting in his lap.

Tom's only regret was that the camera was back at the apartment. *Hell with it—I can use the camera on the cell. Quality won't be as good, but this lady's hotness will shine right on through.*

Technically, nobody was supposed to be on the site at night, but it wasn't like there was a guard or anything. And Tom had never had sex on a site before. Hell, it never even *occurred* to him. That was work, after all, and sex was play. You didn't mix those two.

Or at least, that was what Tom had thought. Whatever.

Brushing aside the plastic tarp that protected the superstructure from the elements, Tom led Teresa into the foundation, which involved a quick jump down into a recessed part of the ground. Tom could've helped her down, but he liked the way her boobs bounced when she jumped.

Tearing his eyes away from that fantastic sight, Tom turned around and indicated the foundation with his hands. "This is where the basement's gonna be. We—"

"What're those?"

Looking back at her, Tom saw that Teresa was pointing at something on the floor. Following her finger, Tom looked and saw what looked like the end of a bone sticking up out of the ground.

"Okay, that's weird." Walking toward the bone, he knelt on one knee and brushed away some of the dirt around it.

"Maybe somebody's buried here!"

Tom had no objection to that. That'd mean a police investigation, which would delay construction, which would mean Tom would get to spend more time living on Key West and finding more women to sleep with and stick it to Missy.

So he started brushing aside more and more dirt, only to discover *a lot* of bones.

"Wow," Teresa said. "This is *amazing.*"

"Yeah." Tom saw the look of rapture on Teresa's face and wondered if he was going to miss out on getting laid because she suddenly went nuts over a pile of bones.

The more the two of them dug—and Tom had to admit to being impressed, as Teresa had a nice manicure, which she was seriously damaging by helping him unearth the bones—the more bones they found. A lot of duplicates, too—he saw several hands, a few skulls, and a lot of other bones that he didn't know what they were.

"Maybe it's an Indian burial ground!" Teresa said with a gasp.

God, I hope not. That would shut the site down. If some Seminoles or whatever were buried here, then the tribes would get into it, and it'd be a huge mess. Probably delay construction for years.

"What's that noise?" Teresa asked.

Tom hadn't heard anything, but once she asked the question, he noticed a low hum. "I dunno."

Then, suddenly, he felt *tired*. Like all the energy had drained from his limbs. It was the way he felt after a day of double overtime, only a thousand times worse. *Jesus, I just want to sleep.*

He could barely keep his eyes open, and he tried to look at Teresa, who also looked drowsy. *What the hell's going on?*

Teresa started glowing, then her cat eyes got really wide, and her mouth opened, and her skin—

Her skin was getting all wrinkly! *What the—?*

Glancing down at his own hands, he saw that they had become withered and weak and sagging on the bone. *This isn't possible!*

Teresa was screaming now, her cheeks having grown sallow, her face dried out and plastered to her skull. Under the tank top, he could make out her clavicle and ribs, and her boobs were sagging down . . .

Tom tried to scream, but he couldn't muster the energy. He was just so tired—he couldn't lift his arms . . .

The last thing he heard was a phrase in a language he'd never heard before, but somehow he knew that the words meant: "At last!"

TEN

"Anyone ever told you that you got the most *amazing* blue eyes?"

The truthful answer to that question was "no," since Dean didn't have blue eyes, and wasn't entirely sure how anyone could think he *did* have blue eyes—but when the person asking was as hot as this girl was, Dean just gave her a big smile, and said, "Why thank you!"

Besides, he could shout that more easily than he could shout an explanation that his eyes were actually hazel. He was sitting at the bar in Captain Tony's Saloon, his ears grooving on the house band that was doing classic rock covers at a very loud volume, and his eyes were taking in the beauty of the girl who'd just complimented him.

Once it got late enough, he and Sam would go back to Eaton Street and check out the tour company where those two people were killed. Sam had done his laptop mojo thing back at the Naylor House while Dean fixed the EMF reader, and learned that the two who were killed had their heads bashed in, but there was no evidence of who killed them on either body—except for a thread from one of the dolls that was kept in the turret. According to Nicki and Bodge, the legend in that house was that the doll was possessed by a spirit.

If that spirit had been supercharged by whatever zapped Naylor and Hemingway, it could well have been responsible. Especially since the threads from the doll were found on both corpses, but only one of them—the woman—was in the turret with the thing. The guy was killed downstairs, nowhere near the doll.

But that was for later. For now, Dean had dragged Sam—kicking and screaming—to an open-air place around the corner from Sloppy Joe's.

"You see, Sammy," he had explained, as they turned off Duval onto Greene Street, "Sloppy Joe's is a big-ass tourist trap—dining out on the fact that Hemingway went there. Drinks cost too much, there's a cover charge . . . No, you want a good time, you come to the site of the *original* Sloppy Joe's." He had pointed at the outer entrance as they'd approached. "Captain Tony's. Guy who owns it used to be mayor, and they built it around a couple of trees, one of which used to be the town's hangin' tree."

"Really?" That had, unsurprisingly, piqued Sam's geeky interest.

Inside, the bar was a large rectangle, with seats on all four sides and two bartenders working it. To the left of the bar was a semiopen space—broken by the hanging tree—with small round tables and chairs. In front of the bar was an open dance floor facing a stage, where a five-piece band had just finished playing "House of the Rising Sun," and moved on to "Like a Rolling Stone." To the right of the bar was a narrow pathway, and also a short staircase leading down to the "pool pit," an area filled with two pool tables and televisions showing ESPN. The owners discouraged playing for money, so Dean had never much seen the point in using the tables. Besides, the smaller, nonregulation tables always messed with his game.

The walls were covered floor to ceiling with stapled-on business cards, as well as the occasional bra. (Upon seeing the bras, Sam had said, "Oh, so *that's* why you wanted to come back here.")

It was past two-thirty in the morning, and one of the bartenders had announced last call. Dean was nursing a beer, while his companion—whose name he could not for the life of him remember—ordered a final gin and tonic.

The band finished "Like a Rolling Stone" with a lengthy riff on a single chord before finally ending it. Amid the applause of what was left of the crowd, the singer said, "We got one more, then we're callin' it a night. We are Grande Skim Latte, and we thank you for seein' through the night with us. Good night, Key West!"

More applause, then they broke into "Devil with the Blue Dress."

"So Dean," the girl said, "how long you in Key West for?"

Dean had really been hoping that she couldn't remember his name, either. Her long, straight brown hair was tied back in a ponytail, and she had doelike brown eyes under thin eyebrows, and full lips. Her hot pink short shorts showed off an amazing pair of legs, and her flip-flops left her toes exposed, painted in the same hot pink, with sparkles. Her fingernails were painted to match. Her white T-shirt was about half a size too small, not that Dean was complaining, especially since he could clearly make out the lace bra underneath.

In answer to her question, he said, "Not sure. Me and my brother—we tend to play things by ear. See what comes up."

"I can think of a few things that might," she said, putting a hand on his leg, fingers inching to his inner thigh.

Smiling, Dean asked, "How long *you* in Key West for?"

"Through the weekend."

Yahtzee. "Look, I gotta take care of some stuff

tonight—and maybe the next few days. Why don't we meet back here Saturday night?"

She leaned in close enough that Dean could smell the gin on her breath, mixed with sweat and a rose-scented perfume. It was actually a pretty hot combination. "What if I find a better offer between now and then?"

Grande Skim Latte had segued into "Good Golly Miss Molly," and Dean realized that they were duplicating the medley that Bruce Springsteen performed at the *No Nukes* concert back in the seventies. "Jenny Take a Ride" would be next.

Dean leaned in even closer, putting his mouth near her ear. "Trust me, you won't find one."

The girl smiled widely, gulped down her final gin and tonic, and reached into her fanny pack, pulling out a business card. "My cell's on there. Call me or text me anytime if you decide you can't wait until Saturday. Or maybe you'll get lucky, and I'll be here Saturday."

Dean took the card and saw that her name was Susannah Hallas. Pocketing it, he said, "I'll see you Saturday, Susannah."

"I like a confident man," she said, cupping his chin with her hand. "By the way, next time, wear something a little less Yankee. You look like a tourist in those jeans." She got up and headed out, casting a seductive glance back at him before departing onto Greene Street.

Now I just have to hope the job's done by Saturday. I knew this place was a good-luck charm. And if the job wasn't done before then, he could always call her. Or, if he had to, text-message her, though that was a form of communicating Dean had never been able to wrap his mind around. He agreed with what Gin Rummy on *The Boondocks* cartoon said: Nobody ever typed anything worthwhile with their thumbs.

Dean was grateful that Yaphet had called Dad's phone. His and Sam's one trip had been too short to enjoy properly, but the trip with Dad had been fantastic.

He had forgotten about the Key West "uniform": T-shirt and shorts, and either flip-flops or sandals. After his and Dad's trip, Dean was convinced that nobody on the island even *owned* a pair of socks. He and Sam had the T-shirt part down, leaving their flannel button-downs in the Impala trunk, but they were still sticking with jeans and actual shoes with socks. Glancing around Captain Tony's, he noticed that he and Sam were the only people in the place whose legs were not exposed to the world.

The band did indeed go into "Jenny Take a Ride," then finished off with a final refrain of "Devil with the Blue Dress." Dean clapped along with everyone else, making a mental note to dig out his tape of *No Nukes* to play in the Impala.

While Grande Skim Latte tore down, Sam ambled up from the pool pit, where he'd been watching the games. Dean knew that Sam was bound and determined to get Dean out of the deal with the crossroads demon, having already gone so far as to shoot the demon with the Colt. Dean certainly appreciated the sentiment, but he wasn't losing all that much sleep over it. The way Dean saw it, he'd cheated death twice. First when he was electrocuted and brought back by that preacher in Oklahoma, who'd unknowingly killed someone else in Dean's place. Then again when Dad sacrificed himself to the yellow-eyed bastard to bring Dean back from the injuries sustained in a car crash. Ever since the electrocution, Dean had been living on borrowed time, time that had now been stolen from two other people who, frankly, deserved it more than Dean.

So this time, *he* was the one making the sacrifice. Paying it forward, in a way. That poor bastard in Oklahoma and Dad had both died so that Dean would live, so now Dean would die so that Sam would live. He fingered the amulet around his neck, a charm that Sam had given him during one of the many Christmases that they had spent alone, Dad off on a job somewhere. Dean had been spending his life protecting Sam, and he wasn't about to let Sam's being stabbed in the back make a failure out of him.

Still, Sammy was gonna try to save him. Dean wouldn't be Dean if he didn't do everything he could to keep his little brother safe, and Sam wouldn't be Sam if he didn't try to do whatever he could to beat the odds and get that happy ending that they never seemed to get.

"So, win any games?" Dean asked as Sam came over, a quarter-full cup of beer in his hand.

Sam snorted. "Right. You know I suck at that game."

"Yeah, but I like hearing you admit it out loud."

"Nah, I was just watching." Sam gulped down the last of his beer.

Grinning, Dean said, "You pool voyeur, you."

"Get anywhere with the girl in the hot pink shorts?"

The grin widened. "Yup. We're meeting back here Saturday. I figure we'll have this taken care of by then."

"Hope so." Sam set down his cup. "Ready to make with the mad lockpicking skillz?"

"Let's do it," Dean said, gulping down his own beer.

This late on a Wednesday night after a holiday weekend, Duval Street wasn't terribly crowded. That didn't mean it was empty—drunken revelers were still wandering about in groups of two or more, plus the occasional solo pedestrian. Most of the bars had closed up, and Dean had to admit, it was *weird* seeing the open-air places with their gates and windows shut. Open, they looked like inviting places to come sit. Closed, they actually looked like buildings.

When they passed the Bull and Whistle, Dean was surprised to see that Yaphet was still there.

"Hey, dudes!" he said. "I was hopin' you two'd show up. There's been, like, a disturbance in the Force."

"What do you mean?" Sam asked.

"Construction site down on South Street. Some seriously bad shit happenin' down there, if you'll pardon my French. Two people went in, didn't nobody come out. Cops're there now, but they won't be there forever, y'know?"

"Hey," Sam said, "you know a cop named Van Montrose?"

"Yeah. Seminole dude. He's a cool cat, for a pig."

"You trust him?"

Yaphet shivered. "Well, y'know, he's a pig, man. Can't trust the fuzz. But for fuzz, he ain't bad."

Dean figured that was as good an endorsement as they'd get. He looked at his brother. "You wanna check that out instead of the tour company?"

"We should do both," Sam said. "Maybe split up, take one each?"

"Nah, that never works. Every time we split up, things get bad."

Sam shrugged. "When we stick together, things get bad, too. What difference does it make? It's not like this is a horror movie, where splitting up leads to instant death."

"Dude, our *lives* are horror movies." Dean held up a hand, cutting off another protest. "Fine, whatever, we stay together. Let's do it." Looking down at Yaphet, he said, "Keep it cool, Yaphet."

"Right on, brother," Yaphet said, holding up a fist. "Hey, Sammy, you check out my poem yet?"

Suddenly nervous, Sam said, "Uh, no, not yet."

"Well, lemme know what you think when you do, 'kay?"

"Sure thing," Sam said in his best bullshit voice.

As they walked off, Dean said, "Poem's that bad, huh?"

Sam winced. "Worse."

They walked up to Eaton, which was even more deserted than Duval. After a quick trip to their rooms to retrieve the EMF, picklocks, flashlights, and their weapons, they crossed the street to the house with the turret. The occasional person wandering by was enough to make Dean suggest they try the back entrance first, but that notion was quickly kiboshed as that entryway had been sealed.

The front door, though, was just locked and alarmed. Which was good as far as it went, but the front entrance was completely exposed to the street.

As Dean knelt to pick it, he said, "Do me a favor and stand in front of me and make yourself tall."

"I don't need to *make* myself tall, Dean, I *am* tall," Sam said in that tone he always used when he gloatingly reminded Dean that, for all that Sam was the "little" brother, he had a good three inches on Dean. Sammy'd been using that tone since hitting his growth spurt at age fourteen and shooting past Dean on the height chart. Back then, of course, Sam provided those reminders approximately once every five minutes. "Hey," teenaged Sam would say, "can I borrow your jacket? Oh, wait—it's too *small* for me!"

Now, though, he needed his brother to be the Incredible Hulk. "Just widen your shoulders or something."

It took almost a minute to pick the lock, then another ten seconds to switch off the alarm.

Once that happened, the two brothers moved almost as a unit, training that was drilled into them by their ex-Marine father from the time that both boys were old enough to be trusted with firearms, one covering the other while the latter moved in a bit, then the former moving while being covered.

Within a minute, both brothers were sure the ground floor was clear, and Dean closed the door. "We should try to find where each of them was killed."

"I'm gonna go out on a limb and say one of 'em

was right there." Sam was pointing his finger at the gift shop that was in the back of the ground floor, where a display unit had been shattered from the top, as if something had fallen on it. Most of the top shelf and some of the second shelf were broken, too. It was, Dean thought, consistent with someone falling onto the thing. Looking closely, he saw that some of the glass fragments had blood on them, as did the shelves. He also noticed that there was a slot for a third shelf, but it was missing— probably at the local crime lab.

Sam was looking at the Florida license plates with people's names on them and other junk. "People really buy this crap?"

Dean shrugged. "Tourists." Pulling the EMF out of his pocket, he closed his eyes, winced, then turned it on. When he didn't feel it spark or hear it explode, he opened one eye.

It was working fine. He'd recalibrated it to handle the higher levels Key West ghosts were giving off these days, and it looked like he'd done so properly. Opening the other eye, he told Sam, "Same thing we got at Hemingway—EMF's off the freakin' scale."

"The other body was upstairs," Sam said.

Looking around, Dean saw the winding staircase that led up to the turret. "Let's go."

Again, John Winchester's training kicked in, and the pair of them moved up the stairs the same way they'd entered the building. The wooden stairs creaked as they progressed, but there was nothing to be done about it. *Hell, this is the HQ for a haunted-house tour. Of* course *the stairs creak.*

Dean moved up around one bend, then covered Sam as he went around the next one, eventually making their way to the top of the spiral, where a big wooden door greeted them. Dean noted that the EMF readings were spiking. "I think our little dolly of doom is definitely up here."

Pocketing the EMF, Dean raised his shotgun, standing at the left of the big wooden door. Sam took the other side, his own sawed-off at the ready.

Dean held up three fingers, then two, then one—then they burst in.

The room was quiet—and kind of weird. It was filled with tiny furniture—too small to be used by anyone fully grown but not small enough for the average toy. "It's like a dollhouse for Paul Bunyan's action figures," Sam said as he hunched over in order to enter.

"Yeah, or Billy Barty's place." Dean didn't have to hunch over nearly so much as Sam. With a grin, he added, "If you wanna wait outside while us normal-heighted people look around . . ."

"Hardy har har."

Chuckling, Dean looked around, but saw nothing out of the ordinary, beyond the weirdness of the room itself. Unlike the mess downstairs, all the furniture was neat and orderly. "You sure the girl was killed up here?"

Sam nodded, moving to the right. "That's what the report said." He looked behind him, and said, "Uh, Dean?"

Looking up, Dean saw his brother swing the door partly shut. It was covered in now-dried blood.

"The M.E. report said the woman died of blunt-force trauma to the head causing a subdural hematoma."

Dean blew out a breath. "And the door probably caused the trauma." He shined his flashlight around the room. "So where's the blunt force?"

"What do you mean?"

"Look around—lotsa furnishings, no occupant. Where's the doll?"

"His name's Raymond."

Dean shot a look at his crouching brother. "The doll has a name?"

"Most dolls do."

"And you would know this, how, exactly?"

Sam just gave Dean a *bite me entirely* look. "The doll was a mischievous spirit, according to the legend. It would cause all kinds of problems, and the kid who had the doll would be blamed for it. When the kid grew up, he redid the turret so it would be Raymond's room. The doll's lived up here ever since, but the lore has it that it causes trouble every once in a while."

"Murder's a little more intense than 'mischievous.'"

Sam shrugged as he knelt by the door to peer more closely at the blood. "Yeah, well, Hemingway's spirit didn't used to have a mad-on for cats, either." He squinted at the door. "Geez—there's, like, four different indentations on the door here. And the blood spatter's consistent with that. This wasn't just murder, it was overkill."

"Thank you William Petersen," Dean muttered. "So where *is* Raymond?"

He shined the flashlight everywhere except the window—directly shining the light on the window might alert someone on the street that there was someone in the turret, and they couldn't count on all the island cops being as accommodating as Montrose—but there was nothing. Just itty-bitty furniture.

Then he looked up and pointed the flashlight at the ceiling.

A doll that looked like a monkey with a Beatles wig and a striped shirt was up in the rafters. As soon as the light hit it, it started to hurtle down toward Dean.

Dean raised his shotgun and leapt out of the way, but Raymond changed direction somehow and landed right on Dean, hard enough to knock him to the floor.

Where the hell did this thing get this kind of weight? Dean thought as, once again, his training kicked in and he angled his body so that his shoulder took the worst of the fall to the wood floor.

Sam cried, "Dean!" even as Dean tried to push off Raymond. The doll wouldn't budge, though. Instead, its little hands clamped the sides of Dean's head.

Realizing it was trying to do the same thing to Dean that it had done to that girl, Dean tried to get up, but Raymond's weight was too great. Still, he flexed his neck, pushing his head upward to resist the force of Raymond's iron grip.

Suddenly, the grip was gone, as Sam's workboot collided with the doll hard enough to send it flying. Thinking, *Can't do* that *wearing flip-flops,* Dean clambered to his feet even as Sam—now that Dean was clear of his shot—fired a rock-salt round at the doll.

But it ducked behind one of the chairs, and the rock-salt sprayed harmlessly against the stone wall with a clatter.

Dean pointed to one side of the chair while he moved quickly around to the other side. All hopes of being sneaky were screwed by the damn creaky floor, so unless the doll was deaf, it was gonna know they were coming. Luckily, there weren't too many places to go in this room.

As Sam set up on the far side of the chair, Dean leapt forward, aiming the shotgun at the floor.

There was no sign of the doll. *Where the hell is it?*

"Ooof!" Sam fell to the floor, his gangly arms flailing. Running back around the chair, Dean saw that the doll had tripped Sammy, but his little brother had kept a grip on his shotgun. Sam tried to bring the stock down on the doll's head, but he couldn't get leverage.

Dean ran over to do the same, slamming the wood into the doll's head. That, at least, made it loosen its grip on Sam's leg. Dean quickly backed up just as the doll again launched itself at Dean.

This time, he swung the shotgun like a baseball bat, and it knocked the doll right into the wall next to the window.

As soon as it fell to the ground, Sam, still lying on the floor, shot it. The doll blew apart with a flash of black light, straw and cloth flying all over the place.

"You okay?" Sam asked as he got to his feet.

Dean nodded. "Yeah. Let's hope that the spirit was tied to the doll and blowing it to pieces means it won't come back the way Hemingway threatened to."

Sam blew out a breath. "Let's check that construction site—but Dean? The more I see, the more I think this is a demon, or something worse."

"What, another god?" Dean asked with a cheeky grin as they moved toward the door.

"Maybe. EMF off the charts, spirits acting out

of character—we need to find out who's doing this before things get worse."

"C'mon," Dean said, grateful to be able to stand up straight in the stairwell. "Let's get outta here before someone reports that shotgun blast."

ELEVEN

"No points for originality," Sam muttered, as they got out of the Impala, which Dean had parked across the street from the construction site.

"Sorry?" Dean asked as he closed the driver's side door behind him with a loud thunk.

Sam joined Dean at the trunk. "We're at the southernmost part of the southernmost location on the continental United States. They couldn't come up with something more interesting to name this than 'South Street'?"

Dean shrugged as he double-checked his sawed-off. "Maybe not original, but it's pretty damn descriptive." He closed the trunk. "Feel kinda silly calling it the southernmost part of the 'continental' U.S., though. I mean, it's an island."

They started to cross the street. Sam said, "Dad used to call it 'the lower forty-eight.'"

"Yeah, but Hawaii's south of everything, so it's 'lower' than we are now. That's why you had to qualify the whole southernmost-point crap in the first place."

Sam shook his head. "Why are we talking about this?"

"Dude, you started it."

"Whatever." Sam looked at the site, which was barely lit this late at night. He could hear the flap of crime-scene tape, and his flashlight illuminated the yellow barrier. "Least nobody's guarding the scene. That's pretty *laissez-faire*."

"Key West is big on the whole yeah-whatever-can-I-have-another-beer philosophy. They probably figure no one'll mess with it."

"Yeah, Dean," Sam said with a small smile, "that's what *laissez-faire* means."

Shining his light in Sam's face, which caused him to squint and hold up one hand, Dean said, "I know, dumb-ass, I was *agreeing* with you."

"Fine," Sam said, and Dean lowered the flashlight. Sam blinked the spots out of his eyes and marveled at how Dean still fell into old habits. When they were kids, Sam was always the book-smart one who liked studying, while Dean was more of the type to beat up the nerds, and who hated admitting to knowing anything. Smart made you an outcast, and given their hard-traveling ways, Dean had enough issues in school with that.

So he adopted the jock persona of not caring about learning anything.

That tendency still bled into his personality, to Sam's annoyance, to the point where Dean would profess ignorance on subjects Sam knew damn well he was knowledgeable about. Anything to not be the nerdy kid.

Like any of that crap matters now, Sam thought bitterly.

Thrusting these thoughts out of his head, Sam looked at the site. The work had only just started, with a few girders clawing upward and a tarp over them making it look like a tent.

Pushing the tarp aside, Sam saw that the site was just a big hole in the ground.

"Crap!" Dean cried, even as Sam heard sparking. Whirling around, he saw the EMF was having the same overload it had had in the Hemingway Home and Museum.

"Dude, I thought you fixed that."

"I *did*," Dean said angrily, shutting it off before things got worse. "Calibrated it so that it could handle twice the EMF it could before." Looking around, Dean said, "Whatever we got here's even stronger than Hemingway and Raymond."

Considering that those two spirits had more supernatural energy than average, that didn't bode well.

Putting on a scratchy voice and a British-sounding accent, Dean said, "Look at the *bones*!"

Sam stared at his brother, mouth agape. "What?"

"Dude, *Holy Grail*?"

Finally placing the line as being from *Monty Python and the Holy Grail*, Sam said, "Oh yeah, right."

Dean rolled his eyes. "Funniest movie in the history of the human race, and 'Oh yeah, right' is the best you can do? You sure you're my brother, Sammy?"

Ignoring the dig, Sam instead did as Dean had instructed in his impersonation of Tim the Enchanter. There were indeed bones just under the surface of the hole that was probably going to be the basement of the building.

Jumping down into the hole, Sam looked at the walls of the hole and tried to recall the geology class he'd taken at Stanford. "Dean, if I'm reading these rocks right, this is deeper than they've gone before."

"What do you mean?" Dean asked, hopping down next to him. "And since when do you read rocks?"

"If I'm remembering Geology 101, all of this has been underground for a long time. Which means the previous building didn't have a basement as low as this."

"Katrina, probably," Dean said. "Louisiana got all the publicity, but the entire Gulf Coast got hammered. Whatever used to be here probably got totally wiped out, along with the first few layers of dirt."

Sam nodded. "That follows. 'Cause those bones probably aren't all that recent."

"Cayo Hueso," Dean said. "It means—"

"'Bone Key,' I know," Sam said. At Dean's surprised look, he added, "I went to college in California, remember? You pick up some Spanish."

"Uh-huh. Well, it's called that because when the Spaniards first showed up in Florida, this island was covered in bones. It was occupied by one of the tribes that got wiped out—the Anasazi, maybe?"

Sam shook his head. "They're the Southwest. I'll check it out later."

"Either way," Dean said as he looked around the rest of the site—which didn't take long, as there wasn't much there aside from a few unearthed bones and a whole lot of dirt, "the bones were mostly the tribe's enemies. They probably buried their own people deeper."

"So the bones of dozens—maybe hundreds of members of a long-dead Indian tribe are down here where a demon just raised the spiritual ante."

"Yeah," Dean said. "Not much else here. Whatever the spirit did to those two, that did it for now, but it might be back later."

"We should salt and burn the bones."

Dean shot him a look. "And lemme say again,

Sammy, look at the bones." He said it in his own voice this time, for which Sam was grateful. "Just what's poking out there is at least five different people, and I can't tell how far down it goes—or how far across. Unless we set the whole site on fire, and even if we do, we don't have *that* much salt."

Sam had to agree with his brother; for one thing, there were at least four right hands just in what he could see, as well as five skulls. The usual method was going to be a bit too overt in this case. "And it's not like this place gets a lot of snow, so we're not gonna be able to get the stuff in bulk all that easily."

"Yeah. Let's head back to the B&B, get some sleep, then we'll do the research thing in the A.M."

By the following afternoon, Dean had had enough of the Monroe County Public Library. He and Sam had spent all their time since waking up (close to noon after the long night they had) sitting there, going through various and sundry records while hyped up on Nicki and Bodge's excellent coffee. The library was conveniently located near the Naylor House: three blocks over and one block down on Fleming Street. Dean was handling the construction site and going through the newspapers to see if there were other hauntings—or murders—that might give them a clue as to what was going on. That left Sam to check out the lost tribe.

They broke for lunch, only for Dean to realize, to his great chagrin, that the Hooters on Duval Street was no longer there.

"My heart bleeds for you," Sam said in that snotty tone of his. "C'mon, Bodge recommended a place to me this morning."

"When did that happen?"

"You were sitting right next to me, Dean." Then Sam smiled. "Of course, that was before you had your coffee . . ."

"That explains it, then." They went to a place that was on the second floor. The cute maitre d' showed them out to the balcony, which had a waist-high brick wall and several small metal tables with glass tops, and wrought-iron chairs that dug into your back but managed to be comfortable anyhow. Dean had never figured that one out, but chalked it up to life's little mysteries.

They had a nice view of Duval. While it was much quieter—and sunnier—in midafternoon, there were still plenty of people walking up and down, as the street was full of shops, as well as restaurants, museums, and other stuff. Dean wondered if he'd have an opportunity to get to the beach—though it was a bit chilly for that. While it was a lot warmer than South Dakota, it wasn't quite bathing-suit weather, either.

After ordering a couple of beers and a basket of fried shrimp and fries for the two of them to share,

Dean asked, "So what do you know about our lost tribe?"

"Not much," Sam said with a sigh. "They were called the Calusa, and most of what we know about them is that we don't know much about them. They had a reputation as fierce warriors, which was helped by their tendency to pile up the bones of their enemies."

"Hence, Cayo Hueso," Dean said just as the waitress—who wasn't quite as cute as the maitre d', but was still pretty hot, and was named Paula—brought two bottles. "Thanks."

Sam also said, "Thanks."

Paula gave Dean a big smile—she had *great* teeth—and said, "No problem. *Anything* else you need, let me know."

She walked back toward the kitchen, giving Dean a nice opportunity to see how well her ass moved in her shorts. *Hooters, schmooters,* he thought with a smile.

"What *is* it with you?" Sam asked.

Dean smirked and took a pull on his beer. "Jealous?"

"Please. Anyhow, the Calusa occupied the island for centuries, fighting off the other tribes and the European settlers, but disease wiped them out in the eighteenth century."

Shaking his head, Dean said, "The old malaria-in-the-blankets routine?"

"Nothing *quite* that cold-blooded, but all it'd take is one of them to catch something from a European that they hadn't built any kind of immunity to, and . . ."

"Excellent diagnosis, Dr. House."

Making his little pouty face, Sam asked, "Fine, what'd *you* dig up?"

Taking another sip of beer first, Dean said, "We were right about Katrina. A lot of the places on South Street got pummeled back in '05. The owners sold the lot, the new people decided to build something new. Construction crew's also one short now—one of our two corpses was one of the workers. Other one was a woman from Miami, down here for a getaway."

Paula came by with a big basket filled with breaded shrimp and French fries, as well as a plastic cup filled with tartar sauce. "Thanks again."

"Anything else? Anything at all?"

Under other circumstances, Dean would have several suggestions, but they were on the clock, as it were. "If we think of somethin', we'll let you know."

There were already bottles of various condiments on the table, and Dean immediately grabbed the ketchup bottle and squeezed out the lovely redness onto the fries.

Sam watched him with that stupid little-brother

expression of his. "Want some fries to go with your ketchup?"

"So anyhow," Dean said, popping a ketchup-soaked fry into his mouth, "they only were able to ID the bodies based on their wallets. The bodies were 'unrecognizable.'"

"Well, the library had a wireless network, so I was able to get online," Sam said, indicating his laptop with his head while he speared a shrimp with his fork and dipped it into the tartar sauce. "And they weren't kidding about them being unrecognizable. Their skin was wrinkled and almost mummified. But their hair was still the same as it was in their ID photos."

"That's weird."

"Not really." Sam bit into another shrimp and swallowed it before going on, in full boring-lecture mode. "Despite what TV would have you believe, if you age someone rapidly, their hair *won't* go gray automatically. That's something that can only happen over the course of times as new hair grows."

"Thank you, Dr. Wizard." Dean popped another fry and forked a shrimp of his own. "We need to find the demon that started this. Any word from Bobby?"

Sam shook his head while he chewed. "Left a message, though."

Dean thought a minute while he ate some more,

then washed it down with more beer. "All right, let's go to where that girl was killed. That's where the sulfur was, and I'm willing to bet real money that her blood was used for the ritual that amped up the spirits."

"No bet. But how do we trace the demon?"

Dean scratched his ear. "Most of the demons who got out of the gate have been taking advantage of the whole having-a-body thing. He probably came down here as much for the vacation value as the spiritual energy."

"Not a 'he.' I think we've got a couple," Sam said.

"What?"

"All the witness statements for the killing had the girl leaving the bar with an older couple. The police want 'em for questioning, but they haven't been found yet."

Angrily spearing another shrimp, Dean asked, "What is it with all this share-and-share-alike crap? First the seven deadly sins, then that couple in Ohio, now this. Since when do demons trust each other?"

Shrugging, Sam said, "Maybe they spent so long in hell they formed relationships? I don't know— but I think we have to assume that we've got a pair. And if you're right about them wanting to take advantage of all the pleasures of the flesh, they're probably staying in a luxury hotel."

"The fanciest hotel on the island is the Hyatt on Front." Dean grinned. "Which is, like, a block from where our girl's throat was cut."

"Sounds like a plan."

Susannah Hallas had never considered herself a lightweight before tonight.

She'd been having a great time in the Schooner's Wharf, listening to a local act, an older man with white hair and matching beard, who sounded a bit like Hank Williams, only more relaxed. He did a great song called "Tourist Town Bar" about his job, basically, and an equally hilarious one called "She Gotta Butt," about a woman with a big ass. That song particularly resonated, as the singer's description perfectly matched Susannah's mother.

As sunset rolled around, the white-haired guy was done, and the place just had jukebox music until after sunset, when the evening's band would start playing. Once that happened, Susannah moved on to beer—she'd been sticking with cola until sunset, as she always believed that alcohol was only meant to be consumed when it was dark out.

Then Alberto and Fedra sat at her table—all the other tables were occupied, and she had one all to herself ever since that gay couple left—and offered to buy her a harder drink.

Usually Susannah was good for four gin-and-tonics before the room started spinning and she started losing inhibitions (and, sometimes, articles of clothing), but she barely finished the first one before she started to feel woozy.

"I—I don't feel so good," she said to Alberto, who had the sexiest accent. If he hadn't been there with his wife, she *so* would've been hitting on him. True, she'd promised to get together again with Dean on Saturday, but that was two days away, and as nice as Dean's eyes and smile and biceps were, Susannah was thinking about *tonight*.

Except now she wasn't thinking about much of anything. The Schooner's Wharf was spinning around in circles, and bile built in the back of her throat.

Alberto grabbed her arm in an iron grip, and Susannah practically collapsed into him, letting him bear the brunt of her weight.

"Come," he said, "we will take you to our hotel. We are at the Hyatt."

Susannah said nothing, focusing all her energy on not throwing up all over the Schooner's Wharf floor. She was staying at one of the motels way the hell over on Route 1 right on the other side of the bridge from Stock Island, a choice made by her dumb-ass cousin, whom Susannah kept promising herself she'd never travel with again because she did stupid stuff like that. Why would you come to Key West and stay so far from Duval Street?

In any case, if Alberto and Fedra were staying at the Hyatt, they were only a block away or so. Right now, Susannah wanted to worship at the porcelain god, and a bar bathroom was most definitely *not* where she wanted to do it.

She didn't have any actual memory of walking to the hotel. The ringing of the elevator button echoed in her skull, though. *Christ, it's like I went straight to the hangover.* She kept her eyes shut tight, as the nausea got a thousand times worse when she opened them.

As soon as Fedra put the plastic key into the slot, Susannah ran into the room and went straight for the bathroom. Dimly, she registered that the do-not-disturb card was on the handle (*why, if they weren't in the room?*) and that the bed was propped up against the wall (*usually that means a party*), but mostly she just wanted to get to the damn bathroom already.

Her stomach, perhaps realizing that solace was at hand, chose the moment she crossed the threshold into the bathroom to start heaving. Panicking, Susannah practically leapt to the toilet, throwing the lid up and opening her mouth wide.

But, though she heaved, nothing came out.

She felt a cool hand on her warm neck. It was Alberto. "Come, Susannah, we will take care of what ails you."

God, why can't I throw up? Susannah just knew

that if she could throw up, everything would be better. That was what always happened—mainly because throwing up was the worst thing in the world, and you could only go up from there.

Alberto pulled her to her feet, but she almost collapsed again. Her legs felt like noodles, and if Alberto hadn't caught her, she would probably have cracked her head on the sink or the toilet.

Her feet were dragging on the linoleum floor as Alberto all but carried her back into the main part of the hotel room. Everything was fuzzy, but then her bare feet (*how'd they get bare? what happened to my sandals?*) rubbed against the carpet, and the rough surface against her skin actually forced her to focus a bit.

There were black candles all over the place, and they were all lit. Susannah didn't *think* she'd been in the bathroom long enough for Fedra to have lit all the candles—but then, her sense of time was seriously screwed up.

"Everything will be fine," Alberto whispered gently into her ear as he dragged her over to where the headboard was nailed to the wall. Only then did Susannah notice the thing painted in dark red on it. It looked like—a Star of David? No, that wasn't right. A pentagram, maybe? She'd had a Wiccan roommate named Stephanie back in college, but she couldn't for the life of her remember any of that stuff anymore. Besides, Stephanie kept to herself, just lit a lot of incense, which Susannah had found really nice.

Speaking of which, something was burning, and Susannah suddenly felt the urge to light one of Stephanie's incense sticks.

Jesus, where am I again?

She tried to make her brain work right, but it just wouldn't. Now she was hearing strange noises.

No—that's Alberto. He's chanting something. A long-ago high-school language class—the private high school her fat-assed mother insisted on sending her to actually required students to take *Latin* for God's sake—allowed her to recognize the language he spoke, though she couldn't remember all the words.

Then Fedra turned around and stared at Susannah with dark eyes. No, not just dark eyes, *blacked-out* eyes. No iris, no pupil, just deep, unending *black*.

It was the single scariest thing Susannah had ever seen in her life.

After the brothers had finished lunch (and Dean had gotten Paula's phone number without asking; she provided it with the check), they went back to the Naylor House to change into their suits.

While Dean was changing, Captain Naylor decided to show up. "Pardon me, Mr. Winchester, but may I enquire as to your progress?"

Dean wasn't really inclined to answer, but the captain *had* held up his end of the bargain. "We think a demon has cast a spell that makes spirits like you more powerful."

Naylor recoiled. "To what end?"

"Hell if I know—that's what my brother'n me are gonna try to find out." Tying his tie, Dean said, "Sit tight, Cap'n. We'll get to the bottom of this and send you on to your reward."

"I hope so, Mr. Winchester. Existence has been hellish enough, being tethered to this place for so long, but the awareness I now possess has only intensified that emotion."

Dean actually felt himself feeling sorry for the poor bastard.

Once he was changed, and double-checked the fake ID, he and Sam hopped into the Impala and drove it slowly to the end of Duval, then turned right onto Front, then into the parking lot for the Hyatt Key West Resort and Spa.

"You know," Dean said, adjusting his tie, "we could've just walked it."

"We'd stand out like sore thumbs in these suits on the main drag, Dean," Sam said. "Besides, it's humid as hell."

Dean doubted hell was that humid, but said nothing. *I'll be finding out soon enough,* he thought wryly. But he also saw Sam's point. Easier to convince someone you're a fed if you aren't dripping with sweat. And they'd be less obvious walking on Duval with big sirens on their heads than they would in suits.

Still, driving hadn't been much faster, since it was close to sunset, and everyone was making their way toward the boardwalk for the daily sunset celebration.

As soon as they walked in, someone with a nameplate that read YURI headed right for them. He was wearing a blue button-down shirt, khaki shorts, and moccasins, which was as close to formalwear as Dean had seen on anyone on Key West save him and Sam right now. "Good afternoon, sirs, how may I help you today?"

Flashing his fake ID, Dean said, "I'm Special Agent Danko, this is Special Agent Helm. We're searching for a couple of fugitives, and we think they might be staying at this hotel."

Yuri swallowed, his face going pale. "Oh my God. Are you sure?"

Sam was stone-faced, and spoke in a hard tone. "Very sure, sir. These are cultists who are performing satanic rituals."

"Well, Agent Helm," Yuri said with a smile, "what people do in the privacy of their room is their business."

Ah, Key West, Dean thought, recalling his and

Sam's *laissez-faire* conversation. Sam had probably mentioned "satanic" rituals to get a rise out of the concierge, but nobody here was that uptight.

However, Sammy swung at the curveball like a pro. "These rituals involve murder, sir. That's what makes it *our* business."

Now Yuri blanched. "Oh dear. What can we do to assist you?"

Dean put a reassuring hand on Yuri's shoulder. "It's all right, Yuri, we'll take of this as quietly as we can. Don't want the tourists all upset, we get that."

"Thank you," Yuri said, relieved.

Good-cop-bad-cop may be the oldest trick in the book, Dean thought, *but that's 'cause it keeps working.* "Great, Yuri, great. What we need you to do is tell us if anyone from housekeeping has found any sulfur when they were cleaning up."

That confused Yuri. "Sulfur?"

"It's part of the ritual," Sam said.

"If you'll both wait here," Yuri said, pulling a cell phone out of his shorts pocket, "I'll get the head of housekeeping. Actually," he said as an older woman walked by giving Dean and Sam strange looks, "why don't you follow me?"

All things being equal, Dean would've been happy to people-watch in the lobby, but he didn't want this guy to be any more nervous than he was. *Could be worse—he could find out what's* really *going on*. So he and Sam followed Yuri into a back room, which turned out to be a tiny, cramped office with a wooden desk holding a laptop and an in-box full of papers, a cork bulletin board on the wall with tons of brochures, receipts, and flyers attached to it, and a ceiling fan keeping the air (barely) moving.

A few minutes later, a short, stout, middle-aged Latina woman came into the small office. She stood demurely with her hands clasped in front of her, though Dean read into her facial expression that she'd rather be just about anywhere else.

"Gloria, these two men are from the FBI," Yuri said. "They need to know if anyone has found sulfur in their rooms."

Speaking with a thick accent that sounded Cuban to Dean's ears—not surprising, since Key West was closer to Cuba than it was to Miami— Gloria said, "No, I don't think so."

She sounded tentative, so Dean said, "It'd be a yellowish dust or powder—smells like a burned match."

More confidently, Gloria said, "No, I see nothing like that. Neither do my girls—they tell me things."

Dean had been hoping one of the housekeepers would report it, but it was a long shot. The alternative, which was rapidly becoming necessary, was to go door to door.

However, Sam, bless his geeky little heart, had another idea. "Has anybody refused housekeeping service?"

"Many people," Gloria said. "If they want to be filthy, I can no stop them."

Dean asked, "Anybody who's been staying here since before the new year, and has been consistently refusing it?" No way the demons would want the staff near their ritual knives and bowls and things.

Gloria wrinkled her nose, and said, "Oh, that's 333. Their room must be very very filthy now. It's disgusting."

Yahtzee.

Yuri tapped some keys on the laptop on the desk. "That's the Fedregottis—a married couple, Alberto and Fedra."

"Great," Dean said. "Can we have the key to that room, please?"

Yuri nodded. "Sure. Thanks, Gloria and please—don't tell anyone about this, okay?"

All Gloria did was shrug and walk back out the door. Yuri then led Sam and Dean to an elevator down the hall, away from the main lobby. He fumbled through a large key ring that was in a cargo pocket of his khakis and pulled up a credit-card-style key, which he put into the slot over the elevator call button, then pushed it.

"Uh, look, Yuri," Dean said, again putting his

hand on the man's shoulder, "we appreciate your help and all, but we need to handle this ourselves. A civilian would just get in our way, y'know?"

"Oh!" Yuri actually sounded relieved, which Dean was hoping for. "Yes, Agent Danko, of course." He fumbled through the key ring and pulled up another key. He extricated it from the ring and handed it to Dean. "Here you go. This will open any of the rooms."

"Thanks." Dean entered the elevator, and pushed the button with the 3 on it. As soon as the doors closed, he looked at Sam. "Jesus, 333? How much more obvious could they get?"

"Well, they could've gotten 666, but this hotel doesn't have six floors." Sam dropped the federal-agent act and smirked.

"Yeah." The elevators parted at the third floor, and Dean and Sam wended their way through the back corridors—passing a housekeeping person in the usual maid's outfit that wasn't nearly as skimpy as it was in porno flicks—and came out into the hallway through a door that said STAFF ONLY.

The right room would have been easy enough to find even without the "333" emblazoned on it. Dean knew the smell of sulfur anywhere, and this place was swimming in it. The door handle also had a PRIVACY PLEASE card hanging off it.

"No way housekeeping just missed this," Sam said.

"Yeah—that ain't residue. The Fedregottis're doing something right now." Dean unholstered his nine-millimeter pistol which, like the shotgun, had rock-salt rounds, but unlike the shotgun could be easily brought into a public crowded hotel, especially if one had fake federal ID.

Before they could get within twenty feet of the door, though, Dean saw a sight he wasn't expecting: Captain Naylor.

"What the—? Cap'n, what're you doing here?"

But the spirit didn't respond. Instead, he was striding purposefully down the corridor. Then he turned and went through the door like—well, a ghost.

"Captain Naylor!" Dean called out as he walked, but the spirit was unusually quiet.

"This can't be good," Sam said.

A hand thrust through Dean's chest like the monster in *Alien*. He jumped a couple of inches in the air as the rest of the body came through also: another spirit, this time Hemingway. Despite his threats last time, he showed no interest in Sam or Dean.

"That's Truman," Sam said, pointing to the other end of the hall. Dean followed his gaze and saw someone who sure looked like the picture of the guy who held up the newspaper headline DEWEY DEFEATS TRUMAN.

Undoing the safety on his nine-mil, Dean took

up position in front of the door. Sam did so on the side of the door and nodded to Dean, who slid the key Yuri had given him into the door.

Unfortunately, while the little green light went on to indicate that the door had unlocked, the door wouldn't open. Based on the resistance Dean was getting, the Fedregottis had bolted the door shut.

So Dean kicked the door instead.

It still didn't budge.

Snarling, Dean kicked again, this time putting a dent in the door, but not opening it.

On the fifth kick, accompanied by a scream of rage, the door finally flew open.

Sam burst into the room, quickly followed by Dean, who said, "Hate to interrupt this meeting of Dead People Anonymous, but the neighbors are complaining."

Even as he spoke, he took in the room. The king-sized bed had been lifted upright and propped against the wall to make more room—though the headboard was still in the wall, as it was built in, but their demons had made use of that, turning it into an altar. It was painted in blood with an upside-down pentagram. Black candles lit the room, with help from the sunset that streamed in through the large window.

Standing in the center of the room were a man and a woman, both with olive skin that had been well tanned in the tropical sun. He was tall and skinny, with a big nose and graying hair; she was curvy, with well-teased dark hair and nice cheekbones. The bodies no doubt belonged to the real Alberto and Fedra, but were occupied by a couple of scum-sucking demons, whom Dean would be more than happy to send back to hell.

The spirits were standing in a circle around the Fedregottis. Each new spirit that entered—and Dean only recognized some of them—filled in a gap between two others.

Lying on the floor was a girl with her throat sliced open, the wound parallel to her chin, making it look like she had a second mouth. The innards of her neck were clearly visible thanks to there being almost no blood. Dean's expert eye detected that the carotid had been severed, but—just like the other girl—the blood was gone.

When his eyes moved past the neck, Dean recognized her, from the doe eyes that were now staring blankly at the ceiling to the great legs.

It was Susannah, the girl he met at Captain Tony's.

TWELVE

The couple had been perfectly willing to follow Azazel.

The pair of them found each other in the pits. Their pairing provided no comfort or solace—those weren't permitted in hell—but their suffering was lessened when together. True, it was only in the sense that you suffer less when you were stabbed in the shoulder than when you were shot in the gut, but one took what one could get. They'd been in the pits long enough to have forgotten their own names, and had never taken on new demonic names of their own.

When Azazel had revealed his plan, the couple signed right up. A chance to run amok on Earth after centuries of torment? That was way too good an opportunity—made better, as always, by being able to share in the chaos with each other.

At the appointed time, the couple showed up

near the gate, and they waited—and waited. Azazel's plan didn't really have a time frame, despite
the demon's urging not to be too late arriving at
the doorway to Earth. They had to wait for the
human who would lead them, direct them, show
them the way—the field general for their war on
order and life.

But when the gate finally did open, and they
burst out into the world, there was no field general, and no Azazel. Well, actually, they were both
there, but they were dead. The human had been
shot and killed, his lifeless eyes staring toward
a heaven he was now guaranteed to be excluded
from. As for Azazel, there was no trace of him.
The meat puppet he'd been using lately also lay
dead, and the stink of sulfur and cordite meant
that the Colt had been used. It didn't take long
to learn who had done the deed: the sons of John
Winchester. The couple could smell them—the
older one, Dean, stank of the crossroads demon to
whom he'd sold his life, and the young one, Sam,
had been one of Azazel's chosen.

Without a human or an elder demon to guide
them, everyone went crazy.

But the couple decided to take a vacation. After
all, they were on Earth again, for the first time
in millennia. Why not kick back and enjoy themselves?

So they found a couple of meat puppets who

were in the midst of the latest in a series of knock-down drag-out arguments. Alberto Fedregotti had been (once again) cheating on his wife Fedra, and Fedra had (once again) caught him, this time with one of his coworkers. There had been shouting and acrimony and violence, and then make-up sex, and the Fedregottis' free range of fierceness and negativity and angry passion drew the couple like moths to a flame.

Once the two demons took over the Fedregottis, they went south and east to a place that was known for being relaxing. A place to rest and recuperate after century upon century of torment.

After a time, though, just taking it easy wasn't enough. Their very presence on this island was heightening the spiritual activity—which was already greater than usual for this plane of existence—so they decided to spruce things up a bit. Have a bit of fun. A little vacation was never a bad thing, but they *were* demons, after all. So they changed hotels again—the Hyatt was their ninth—and enacted a plan.

Like all the best things in life, the ritual worked most efficiently with human blood. On this island, it was ridiculously easy to find impressionable young people who were happy to let you pay for their drinks. First there was dear Megan, trying desperately to build a life away from her family, living in a constant state of delicious fear.

And then there was Susannah, footloose and fancy-free and totally oblivious to the dangers of the world. It had been a pleasure to slit her throat, oh yes it had.

Using the power of Susannah's life, and by the light of the black candles made from the fat of dead humans, Alberto and Fedra brought all the spirits of Key West to them. It was sunset, which was not only the ideal time for the ritual, it was also when there would be crowds of people coming off the boardwalk after watching the sun go down. Innocent, happy, carefree souls just waiting to be demolished.

One by one, the spirits came. The writer who had lived on the island, the bartender who died in a hurricane, the drowned scuba diver, the president who had vacationed here, the many captains and sailors who had worked on wreckers, the treasure hunter whose mantra of "today's the day" eventually came to pass, the shipping magnate who died on vacation, saying it was the best time of his life, and so many others.

Even as they entered, even as Alberto continued the incantation that would bend all the spirits to their will, Fedra heard something. A banging on the door. They had taken care to mask their incantations prior to this. However the "magic" of the power of suggestion was generally enough, provided by simply displaying the words PRIVACY

PLEASE on a piece of plastic that hung from the door handle. No one had disturbed them since they checked in last week.

Another banging, and this time the door splintered and dented. Alberto was still holding the vessel containing Susannah's blood and chanting. Fedra moved toward the door; they could ill afford an interruption now. She walked through the ever-growing circle of spirits who surrounded them and prepared for whatever was trying to get in.

The door flew open and there were the Winchester brothers. "Hate to interrupt this meeting of Dead People Anonymous," Dean said, "but the neighbors are complaining."

"Too bad. They weren't invited," Fedra said. She let her eyes go black so the dear boys knew *exactly* what they were dealing with. "And neither are you."

It took only the slightest manipulation of power to send both young men flying across the room and crashing inelegantly into the far wall, knocking a particularly ugly painting off the wall. Fedra had been meaning to burn it in any case.

Dean tried to reach into the inner pocket of the suit he was wearing, and Fedra focused her mind on his arms, pinning them to the wall behind him. "Ah, ah, ah. No whipping out the Colt." At both brothers' surprised look, Fedra added, "Yes, we know all about your demon-killing gun. You got Azazel with it, you *won't* get us."

"I swear," Dean said, his face a rictus of pain and anger, "I will *end* you."

"Oh, my dear sweet Dean, you ain't seen nothin' yet. Sure, a minor death here, a slit throat there, but we're just getting started." But, to her surprise and annoyance, Dean wasn't looking right at her.

He was looking at the corpse at Alberto's feet, the young girl from the Schooner's Wharf whose blood was in the vessel Alberto had cupped in his hands.

And then she understood. "You know this girl, don't you? My, you *do* work fast. You can't have been in town for more than a day or two, and already you've planted your seed. Unless, of course, you use protection. I should hope so, given the way you sleep around—not that an STD'll be much of a problem for you, what with having only a few months left on the clock. But still, you should be considerate of your bedmates. Who knows *what's* floating around on that little pecker of yours."

Typically for a male human, casting aspersions on his genitalia resulted in anger and frustration, and he pushed harder against Fedra's mind—not realizing that his anger and frustration only served to make her stronger. She wasn't about to tell him that, of course—that took all the fun out of it. Besides, if he knew struggling made her stronger, he'd do something sensible like not struggle . . .

More spirits entered. A few more, and Alberto

could cease, as they'd have more than enough for their purposes.

Then she felt it.

Whirling toward the now-open door, she tried to see what it was she had felt. Since arriving on this island, she and Alberto had both felt the tickle of the dead whose soul essence remained tethered to this place, but this—this was several orders of magnitude more powerful than any of the shades who currently stood in a circle around Alberto.

Sam's arms were moving, and Fedra realized that she'd let herself be distracted. She slammed his head against the wall, dazing him.

"Do you feel it, Alberto?" she asked her fellow demon. They had inhabited these meat puppets for so long that they had appropriated their names for their own. "The one that comes is more powerful than all these shades put together. Oh, what we can do with this."

Alberto, still chanting, simply nodded.

The spirit that entered was taller than any of the others. Male, he wore only a small loincloth made of some manner of animal skin bound at the waist by a belt decorated with human bones—fingers and toes, mostly, with a skull in the center. His black hair fell straight to his rear end, and his face was covered by a wooden mask decorated with an elaborate design of red and white and black. Fedra assumed him to be from one of the so-called

"Indian" tribes that had been wiped out by the Europeans.

The spirit then spoke in the language of his people, which surprised Fedra, as the spell should have kept it docile. "Which of the Three Gods are you who have made us mighty?"

One of the (few) perks of being a demon was that you knew the language of anyone you spoke to, so Fedra was able to answer in kind. "Other direction, actually. We are demons who have—"

"Spirits of darkness? Then we have no use for you. We are the Last Calusa, and we reject your gift." And then the spirit raised his arm.

"Alberto . . ." Fedra said, warning in her voice. This should not have been happening. The spell should keep the spirits from acting of their own accord. Speaking was one thing, but none of them should be moving without express orders from Alberto or Fedra.

"S'matter, lady," Dean said, "can't keep a rein on all your horses?"

Ignoring Dean's barb, Fedra walked back through the circle of spirits, grabbed Alberto's hand, and joined him in the chant.

The Last Calusa stumbled, then, and straightened up a moment later, quiet as the others.

But before he could join the circle, he stopped. The mask that covered his face quivered.

Then he reared his head back and screamed.

Light flashed throughout the hotel room. A mighty wind came out of nowhere and extinguished the black candles. The Last Calusa's scream grew louder and louder.

Fedra tried to continue chanting, but the wind was now pounding into her meat puppet's face. She clasped Alberto's hands and chanted more intently, more loudly, hoping to get this spirit under their control as they had the others.

The Last Calusa stopped screaming and straightened, raising his hands toward the two demons.

An invisible force sent the demons flying against the headboard, smearing the blood that made up the reversed pentagram.

The spell was broken. The other spirits looked about in confusion. Some disappeared. Some ran. Others stayed and looked befuddled.

Again, the Last Calusa gestured.

Demons lived in hell, so they were used to pain. Still, it had been a long time since Fedra felt pain such as what the Last Calusa was inflicting upon her and Alberto. This wasn't just meat-puppet pain, for demons were immune to such trivialities. No, the Last Calusa was striking at their demon essence, which shouldn't have been *possible* for a mere spirit.

But this obviously wasn't just a "mere" spirit, Fedra realized, as the Last Calusa's anger pounded into her. *And worse, we made it* more *powerful . . .*

The report of two pistols echoed through the room, and Fedra saw that the Winchester boys were using their silly rock-salt rounds to try to disrupt the Last Calusa.

It didn't work, of course, but it did distract the Last Calusa long enough for Fedra to break his hold on her and try to strike back.

But the Last Calusa merely said, "We are not impressed." He gestured, and Dean's and Sam's pistols flew across the room. Then he gestured again, and Alberto screamed.

Fedra had thought herself beyond fear, but that was before she heard Alberto scream. Demons weren't supposed to scream. Demons were supposed to *provoke* screams.

A pit opened in the core of Fedra's demon essence, as if something had been ripped from her very being.

Then the Last Calusa spoke once again. "This will all end soon. We will have our vengeance."

With that, he and all the remaining spirits just disappeared, leaving Fedra alone with the Winchester brothers.

But not with Alberto. She grabbed him, shook him, but he did not respond.

"Alberto! *Alberto!*"

She couldn't *feel* his presence. They'd been together for millennia, and only now did she realize that he was always there, not just physically, but mentally and even, bizarrely, spiritually. Demons weren't supposed to have soul mates—mostly by virtue of not having souls—but apparently Alberto was hers.

And he was gone. She hadn't been aware of this connection between them, but now that it was gone, its absence was all she *could* feel.

"He's gone."

She heard the click of a safety being taken off a pistol. "One down, one to go."

Whirling around Fedra slammed Dean Winchester into the wall. He kept his grip on the Colt, but Fedra pressed his arm against the wall so that the muzzle was facing the window. Then she looked at Sam, who was making as if to rush her. "Take *one step*, Sammy boy, and Dean fulfills his end of the bargain half a year early."

Fedra saw fury in both brothers' eyes, but she didn't care.

Alberto was *dead*. Someone had to pay for that.

At first, Fedra was ready to kill these two upstarts out of revenge, but a moment's reflection made her realize that they were not her enemy. Well, not her *primary* enemy. The Winchester family was fairly high on demonkind's most wanted list, but right now Fedra's main concern was the Last Calusa.

So she used her meat puppet's mouth to say words she never imagined she'd have cause to say to Sam and Dean Winchester.

"I need your help."

THIRTEEN

"You have *got* to be freakin' *kidding* me!"

Dean said the words, though he spoke for both brothers. Sam stood watching the demon-possessed body of Fedra Fedregotti. Her face was curled in a rictus of fury, and tears streaked down mascara-stained cheeks, coming out of the all-black eyes that were the common symbol of demonic possession.

Sam wanted desperately to wipe that expression off her face, but as long as she had Dean pinned, he didn't dare risk moving.

At least not yet.

"Listen to me," Fedra said. "That—that *thing* is incredibly powerful. It's not just a single spirit, it's the collective spirit of an entire tribe."

Needing to keep her talking while he tried to figure a way out of this, Sam said, "The only reason it's incredibly powerful is because of the spell you and Alberto cast."

Fedra whirled on Sam, and he saw true anguish in her face. "Don't you *dare* speak his name! We were together for millennia, and he's dead. We were supposed to live forever, and he's *dead*!"

"Sam didn't speak *his* name." Dean's voice was strained, as he was pushing hard against Fedra's power. "He spoke the name of the poor bastard your not-so-immortal-as-you-thought demon possessed. And that's one of about a billion reasons why we wouldn't help you if you were the last demon on Earth, up to and including that girl lying dead on the floor."

"I cannot defeat the Last Calusa by myself—and neither can you." Fedra looked down at the corpse of Alberto. "But together, we can do it. You're the legendary Winchester boys. Sam was Azazel's chosen one, and Dean, you *killed* Azazel. If we collaborate . . ."

To Sam's delight, Dean continued to strain, and he was actually making some headway. Considering that she had completely immobilized both Sam and Dean before, the Last Calusa had obviously taken a lot out of her. They needed to press that advantage, so Sam kept her talking. "Why would we work with one of your kind, exactly? You aren't known for being the most trustworthy of partners."

Fedra smiled viciously. "I don't expect you to trust me, Sammy, but we have a mutual enemy—or do you think that the Last Calusa is just going to scare the tourists? He's already killed two humans and one demon, and you *know* it's not going to stop there. His last words were—"

"About vengeance, I heard." Sam did not look directly at Dean, instead keeping eye contact with Fedra while Dean struggled.

His words apparently surprised her. "You understood what he said."

"Yup." It had surprised Sam, too. The Last Calusa wasn't speaking English, but Sam found that he'd understood everything he said. Presumably, Dean did as well, which meant that the Last Calusa was powerful enough to allow himself to be comprehended despite speaking a language that had been dead for over two hundred years.

"Then you know that this spirit is probably out to commit murder on a grand scale. Sweet little do-gooders like yourself don't like it when spirits kill people." She tilted her head. "And don't get all holier-than-thou with me about how you wouldn't lower yourself to collaborate with a demon. You've been working with one for months now."

Sam tensed. *Somehow it just figures that she knows about Ruby.* Then again, Ruby had gone so far as to help Bobby replicate the Colt's ability to kill demons with a single shot—Sam could see how that sort of thing would get around the demon grapevine. Ruby had also dropped some hints about Sam and Dean's mother that were leading Sam down some disturbing roads—sufficiently disturbing that he hadn't yet shared Ruby's revelations (and his own research) on the subject with Dean. First thing was to get Dean out of his deal with the crossroads demon. The rest would come in time.

But that was for later. Right now, he just had to say, "I didn't ask for Ruby's help, and I didn't want it."

Fedra actually sniggered at that. "Oh really? You didn't *want* her to save your pretty little ass, huh? 'Cause without her help, you'd both be worm food about now. And if I didn't need the two of you right now, you'd both be—"

"Ooof!" That was Dean, who had finally broken free of Fedra's will, which caused him to fall to the floor.

From his prone position, Dean raised the Colt.

"We'll talk later," Fedra said. Then she leaned her head back and expelled black smoke from her mouth toward the ceiling, which then zipped out into the hallway.

Pounding the floor with one fist, Dean cried, "Dammit!"

Sam, however, was running over to the woman, who had collapsed onto the floor with the departure of the demonic essence. Her eyes were wide with shock, and she was making gurgling choking noises.

Kneeling beside her, Sam said, "It's okay. We'll get help."

She grabbed Sam's arm in an iron grip and stared intently at him, making more choking noises, but unable to speak. "Hkkk—hkkk—"

Then the grip loosened, and Fedra's head collapsed onto the floor with a hollow thunk. The light went out of her eyes, which now stared blankly at the ceiling.

Dean had gotten to his feet and walked over to Alberto, and checked his pulse. "This one's gone, too." He got up. "Let's blow this pop stand, Sammy—last thing we want is to be around when Yuri finds out there's three dead bodies in here."

"Yeah." Sam didn't like the idea of just leaving the Fedregottis or Dean's friend from Captain Tony's to lie there on the floor. But the corpses would prompt questions that "Agents Danko and Helm" were in no position to answer. "You okay?"

"I'm fine." Dean gave Sam his trademark smirk. "Didn't even really hurt much."

Sam knew that the smirk usually went side by side with bravado, but he was willing to let it go. They snuck down the back stairs and out a fire exit, dashing to the Impala. "Remember what I said before about not wanting to know what stage three is?" Sam said.

"Yeah." Dean loosened his tie and climbed into the driver's seat.

Sam took out his Treo as he approached the passenger door. "I'm gonna give Bobby a call, bring him up to speed."

Dean nodded as he started the car.

"Hey, Sam," Bobby said after the second ring. "'Fraid I ain't had no luck findin' a spell that'd hype up a spirit like that."

"We've actually moved past that," Sam said. As Dean inched down Duval, Sam filled Bobby in.

"Jesus," Bobby said, "the Last Calusa?"

"You know about the Last Calusa?" Sam repeated the spirit's name for Dean's benefit.

"I know what it's supposed to be, yeah. It's a spirit that's infused with the life essence of the *entire* Calusa tribe, and it's out for vengeance on the rest of the world for living while they all died. If the lore's right, this is a majorly powerful spirit."

"Great. And now it's even *more* majorly powerful."

"Lemme dig through my books, see if I can find some specifics. I'll call you back."

"Thanks, Bobby." He ended the call and pocketed his phone. "Looks like Fedra was right—it's a vengeance spirit with a mad-on for anyone who isn't a Native American. Maybe anyone who isn't Calusa."

"Which," Dean said, "since they're all dead, is everyone."

"Pretty much. He's gonna dig into it and get back to us. We need to get down to the construction site. That's where it showed up first, and that's where the bones are."

"We may need to find a barrel of salt," Dean said. "That burn-the-site-down idea is startin' to sound *real* good right now."

"I'm not sure it'd work, Dean. It didn't even blink at your rock-salt round, and it's powerful enough to kill a *demon*. I don't think the usual tricks are gonna work."

"Then we'll think of some *unusual* tricks," Dean said with a snarl. "Because I'll tell you one thing, Sammy, there is no way in hell I'm workin' with that demon."

Smirking, Sam said, "No pun intended."

"Yeah," Dean said with a snort. "Ruby's bad enough."

Sam said nothing in response to that. He knew that Dean had thought Sam's working with Ruby was a huge mistake, and the last thing he wanted right now was to get into the latest in a series of arguments about her.

Within a few minutes, they pulled into the Naylor House driveway. The first thing Dean retrieved out of the trunk was chalk. "Come on. I don't think our lady demon's gonna take 'screw off and die' for an answer, so we better be prepared."

* * *

Shannen Bodell had to keep reminding herself that kicking the client in the 'nads was really bad for business.

Besides, she had worked very hard to get the contract from Kevin Lindenmuth to build a new house on the site of the one that Katrina demolished, and she was damned if she was going to let his attitude jeopardize that.

Especially since the cops were doing everything they could to shitcan the whole thing anyhow . . .

They were standing on the site just after sunset, all the workers sitting around doing nothing, as they had been all day. They were union guys, and they knew they had to show up to work to get paid, even if they didn't actually *do* any work. It was past quitting time, but Lindenmuth had asked them to stay until he and Shannen could work out their "difficulties." This meant overtime, which the workers didn't object to, and Shannen was perfectly happy to bill Lindenmuth for—as well as hitting him with the electric bill for running the work lights they needed after sunset.

"So let me get this straight," Lindenmuth said, wagging a manicured finger toward Shannen's face, the gold bracelets on his wrist jangling with the motion. "Two old farts stumble onto the site and have heart attacks, and for *that*, you have to shut down?" Lindenmuth was wearing a white button-down short-sleeved shirt that probably cost as much as any of Shannen's workers made in a month. He wore pressed khaki shorts and pristine moccasins. It was as close to a business suit as anyone came on Key West.

"No." Shannen spoke very slowly in order to keep her temper under control. "Two people were found dead under mysterious circumstances *and* before they died, they discovered some bones buried under the foundation. The cops are looking into the deaths—"

"I *saw* those two, Ms. Bodell, and they were two very old people who probably just dropped dead when they saw the damn bones."

Shannen refrained from pointing out that one of the corpses was one of her twenty-eight-year-old workers, and the other one was apparently only in her early twenties. The whole thing creeped Shannen out, even though she hadn't really *liked* Tom all that much. His whole revenge-on-his-ex thing had been disgusting enough, but he'd tried to get Shannen in on it. As a woman in a field that was 99.9 percent male, the cavemanlike behavior of construction workers usually was like water off a duck's back to her, but Tom was just *gross* about it.

Still, he had been a good worker when he wasn't being an ass, and even scummy asses didn't deserve to die like *that*. Whatever *that* was.

Not that any of this mattered. "Mr. Lindenmuth, the two dead bodies are almost beside the point. There's the bones to consider."

"Who cares about some old bones?"

"Well, the families of whoever they belong to, for one."

Lindenmuth rolled his eyes. "*Please,* Ms. Bodell. I researched this property *intensely* before purchasing it, and any bones that might be found are so old that I doubt any could obtain the provenance of them."

"They're doing pretty amazing things with science these days, Mr. Lindenmuth. Plus—if they're really that old, they might be Native American bones, which means it ain't just gonna be the cops, it'll be the government. They could shut us down for months—or even permanent, if it's a burial ground or something."

Now Lindenmuth threw up his hands and started pacing. "This is *ridiculous*! I paid *good money* for this lot, money I earned with my hands."

Given how pristine those hands were, Shannen thought it far more likely that the only thing his hands did was sign the checks for the people who actually did the work to earn him that money. She hated rich twerps who tried to pretend that they were like regular people. Hell, even if he'd said he'd earned the money with his brains, she would've respected him more.

But she said nothing, for the same reason that

she didn't kick him in the 'nads. Those hands signed *her* checks, too.

Despite the breeze coming in off the Atlantic Ocean, Lindenmuth's hair didn't move until he ran his hands through it. Even then, it hardly budged. "Look, Ms. Bodell, I appreciate that this is a difficult situation, but I need to have this house finished by the summer."

Shannen winced. "It'll all depend on the bones, Mr. Lindenmuth. But honestly, given how many of 'em there are, the best-case scenario is that we *get back to work* in the summer."

"Seriously? That's ridiculous!"

"I had one job that got delayed by five years." That was farther north in Florida, and the same sort of situation: A hurricane kicked up enough dirt to reveal old Seminole bones. That got caught up in a major political and legal shitstorm, because it turned out that there were all kinds of zoning and building irregularities above and beyond the question of Native remains. Pretty typical for Florida, in truth, but Shannen didn't think that would comfort Lindenmuth all that much, so she didn't go into specifics.

Pulling a cell phone off a belt clip, he wandered off to the sidewalk in front of the site. "Let me make a few calls. No offense, Ms. Bodell, but this requires a particular touch."

"Knock yourself out," she said with a sigh.

She'd been building houses in Florida for ten years now, ever since her husband Rudy passed and left her the business. She'd been running it ten times better than his lazy, unmotivated ass, too. When she inherited it, it was on the verge of bankruptcy. Now it was thriving under the tutelage of the same woman that Rudy had said "couldn't run no construction bidness, no way, no how." After Rudy's death from a heart attack, which occurred while he was eating an entire bucket from KFC, Shannen dedicated her life to proving him wrong.

One of the things she'd done was make connections among the politicians both locally and in Tallahassee. She knew exactly which wheels to grease and when to grease them—which was why she knew that there was nothing to be done, especially if these really were Native bones. Riding roughshod over the tribes was a sure way to get yourself mired in a PR disaster, especially now that so many of the tribes had casino money with which to pay good lawyers and publicists.

Which was why Shannen knew that Lindenmuth's "touch" would do no good. Florida politicos were more than happy to perform illegal acts, but ran like hell from the *appearance* of performing even unethical ones, and being anything but solicitous of a burial ground would torpedo their chances at reelection and, therefore, more graft.

Besides, she knew damn well that the "particular touch" he was referring to was his possession of a penis.

She walked over to her foreman, Chris, who was sitting on a folding chair reading a copy of the *Miami Herald* sports section and muttering, "Goddamn Oklahoma," which meant he was reading about the Fiesta Bowl, in which West Virginia beat Oklahoma 48–28. The other sections of the paper were next to the chair on the ground, weighed down from blowing away by a metal coffee mug.

"How much you lose when West Virginia won?" Shannen asked, knowing that Chris only cared about college football bowl games when he bet on them.

"It ain't that they won—I didn't make the spread. WV won by twenty goddamn points."

"You bet on *more* than twenty?"

Chris shrugged. "Money was better."

"*If* they beat it."

Again, Chris shrugged, then folded the paper and stuck it under the mug with the other sections. "Pays your money, takes your choice. What'd pretty-boy have to say?"

"He thinks he can 'make some calls' so this'll go away."

Folding his meaty arms over his barrel chest, Chris said, "On what planet? He thinks he got suction you ain't got?"

"Probably not, but it can't hurt to try. Maybe he'll surprise us, and we can get back to work."

"Yeah. Hey listen, we're holdin' a little thing for Tom at Captain Tony's later. They're lettin' us have the pool pit for a couple hours."

Shannen nodded. "I'll be there."

"Missy's probably dancin' a jig."

The last thing Shannen wanted to do was discuss Tom's personal life. "Anyhow, I think I'll—"

Suddenly, all the work lights went out, and the site was plunged into near darkness, the only illumination coming from one of the streetlights on South and the crescent moon.

"You forget to pay the bill again, boss?" Chris asked with a smirk.

Since the streetlight was on, it wasn't a blackout, so that was a reasonable question. Except, of course, Shannen *had* paid the bill. So she ignored Chris's smart-ass remark—though she continued to take huge pride in his calling her "boss."

Lindenmuth was staring at his phone. "My cell's dead," he said.

Harry, one another of the workers, had his own phone out. "So's mine."

Another's iPod was equally dead, as were all the other cell phones.

"Okay," Shannen said, "this is messed up. C'mon, let's—"

Then she saw him.

He was a big man, dressed like something out of an old painting of an Indian brave. He had on war paint and a red, white, and black mask over his face, wild black hair, and a belt made of bones. He was wearing a loincloth, and nothing else—except the mask, anyhow. He was pretty hot, actually.

"Sheesh," Chris said. "I thought Halloween was two months ago."

"Great," Shannen said, "the crazies are starting in already." In general, Shannen was supportive of Native causes. After all, they *were* pretty much wiped out, and so had reason to be cranky. But even the most noble causes attracted their share of loonies, and Shannen figured this was some fruit-cake who decided to stir up trouble on the site.

The fruitcake spoke in a scary loud voice. "We are the Last Calusa, and we will have our vengeance."

Lindenmuth was staring in openmouthed shock. "The last *who*?"

Shannen knew all the tribes that currently lived in Florida, and the Calusa wasn't one of them. If she remembered right, they were an old tribe that used to live down here, but they were wiped out a long time ago. So this was a Grade-A fruitcake.

"Once these islands were ours. We were mighty warriors, who lived off the land and sea. Those who tried to fight us died in the trying. Those who enlisted our aid were better for our help. We were the Calusa, and none could destroy us."

Suddenly, Shannen realized that this fruitcake wasn't speaking English or Spanish—the only two languages she knew—but she still understood every word he said.

She also had a Walther PPK .380 in her purse—fully licensed, thank you very much—that she was slowly pulling out, being careful not to move too quickly and spook the fruitcake.

"But then came the outsiders and their sickness, and they brought low the Calusa. Now is the time of our vengeance. You will be the first to die."

When the .380 was fully out, she dropped the purse and held the weapon with both hands, clicking off the safety. "Screw you, pal. Only one's gonna get hurt is you if you don't get your loin-clothed ass off this site."

"We are beyond pain. Beyond suffering. Beyond death. We were taken from this life, and our last act will be for you to join us in the afterworld."

The fruitcake took one step closer to Shannen, and she squeezed the trigger, her wrists bending back a bit from the recoil.

The bullet went right *through* him.

Chris and Harry rushed the guy after Shannen fired, the former wielding a wrench. Harry liked to get his hands dirty.

With a gesture from the Indian, though, Harry and Chris stopped dead in their tracks.

And then they just stopped dead. Their skin got

all wrinkled and dried up and withered. Chris's thick arms were suddenly husks of skin plastered over bone and sagging muscle. Both sets of eyes were sunken and hollow.

Lindenmuth started making incoherent noises, which was more than Shannen was capable of. What she had just seen was impossible.

She squeezed the trigger again and again and again, but again the bullets ran right through him, like he wasn't even *there*.

But she *heard* him. She *saw* him. And he obviously did *something* to Chris and Harry.

Even after the pistol was empty, she kept dry-firing, unable to stop, unable to believe what was happening, unable to process any of this. First Tom, and his messed-up love life. Then Chris and his betting. And Harry, he had a wife and daughter in Tampa, with a college-age son at Purdue in Indiana.

Another gesture from the *thing* that called itself the Last Calusa, and three more guys fell over. Then a few more. Then Lindenmuth.

Then he turned to Shannen.

She could see his eyes under the mask, even in the poor light. They were brown and fierce and angry. Shannen had spent ten years of her adult life married to an abusive bastard, and she remembered the look in his eyes when he was drunk and angry and would start beating on her.

That look in Rudy's eyes had scared her to death, and it was *nothing* compared to what she saw in the eyes of the Last Calusa.

"P-please," she whimpered, lowering the .380. "Please don't."

"It is already done," the Last Calusa said.

Looking down, Shannen saw that her hands were horribly wrinkled, her skin wrinkling and contracting.

"N-no!"

"Yes."

Her suddenly weakened legs unable to hold her weight, Shannen collapsed to the dirt, even as the Last Calusa reared its head back and let out a bone-jarring scream to the heavens.

It was the last thing she would ever hear.

FOURTEEN

When Dean turned left onto South Street from Duval, he quickly slammed on the Impala's brakes.

There were cop cars all around the construction site, more crime-scene tape, and a van from the Monroe County Medical Examiner's Office. At least half a dozen uniformed officers were either wandering around or guarding the perimeter, a few guys were wearing jackets with the same M.E. logo as the van, and there was one guy wearing a tie—the first such Dean had seen on the island not worn by him or Sam.

He also saw at least two dozen bodies covered head to toe in blankets.

Next to him, Sam said, "That can't be good."

Dean looked out the rear window, seeing if the road was clear to make a U-turn, but when he turned back, he saw a uniformed cop heading toward them. "Crap."

Immediately, Dean weighed options. If they ran now, the cops would definitely run the plates, and with all the flashing lights, they'd probably get a good look at the make and model. It was a small island, so it wouldn't take all *that* long to track down so distinctive a car. The plates themselves couldn't be traced back to Dean and Sam, but the fact that they couldn't would be something of a red flag as well, especially since they went to an expired registration (like all the other tags they'd been using since they first got on the feds' radar).

On the other hand, if they played innocent tourist and asked what was happening, they might just get out of there intact. If nothing else, they could say they were headed to the beach, as one reasonable driving route from the Naylor House to the beach on the southern coast was the one they were taking.

Then Dean saw that it was Officer Montrose.

Leaning out the open window, Dean said, "Hi there, Officer."

"Kinda figured you two might turn up. All things bein' equal, I'd let you fellas in to check it out, but I can't, not right now."

"Why the hell not?" Dean asked, surprised at his own outrage given that he hadn't expected to get near the scene in the first place.

Montrose looked over at the scene and pointed at the man wearing the tie. "See the overdressed fella over yonder? That's the chief of police. Last time he set foot in an actual crime scene was in nineteen-and-ninety-two."

"How many dead?" Sam asked.

"Thirty-one. But the reason for the brass band is that one of 'em was the head of the construction company doin' the building here. She's got a *lotta* friends in Tallahassee, if you know what I mean."

"Yeah, so?" Dean asked. Then he got it: "Tallahassee's the capital."

"Friends in high places," Sam added.

"Yup," said Montrose. "And another one of our corpses is Kevin Lindenmuth, who has friends in even higher places—the 'favorites' list on his cell phone includes the private personal numbers of the governor *and* both our senators." He shrugged. "If it was just workin' police at the scene, I'd let you fellas in, but the chief ain't as enlightened. Plus, we're workin' in a fishbowl, so—"

Holding up a hand, Dean said, "We get it." Then he slapped the steering wheel with that hand.

"How'd they die?" Sam asked.

"Same as that couple last night," Montrose said. "Had the life drained out of 'em. M.E.'s still tryin' to come up with a good explanation for it."

"That's a waste of time," Dean said.

"Yeah, but I don't think they're gonna buy 'I don't know.'"

"Maybe not," Sam said, "but we—"

Suddenly the whole area was plunged into near darkness. The headlights and dash lights on the Impala went out even as the ignition gurgled and stopped, and the cop car flashers all went out. Looking up, Dean saw that the one streetlight on the block was also out.

Sam pulled his Treo out of his pocket. "Phone's dead, too."

Immediately, Dean threw open the door to the Impala. Sam did likewise.

"Fellas, I don't think this is a good idea." Montrose's tone conveyed a warning.

Dean just ignored him and his tone as he went back to the trunk. Sam glared at Dean for a second, then turned to face Montrose from over the Impala's roof. "Officer, we're dealing with a spirit that calls itself the Last Calusa. It appears to be the embodiment of the *entire* Calusa tribe, and it's *incredibly* powerful. What's worse, the same thing that amped up all the spirits on this island has made it *more* powerful, and whatever it's about to do next, it's gonna do it *right now*."

Tossing Sam a shotgun, Dean then checked his own weapon to make sure all was well. From the site, he could hear the consternation and complaints of the cops and lab techs as they couldn't make *anything*—not their cars, not their radios, not their techie toys—work.

Then the site grew quiet. Looking up, Dean saw why.

The Last Calusa was back.

"Is it me," Sam asked, "or is he taller this time?"

In the Hyatt, the Last Calusa was about Sam's height. Now, he towered over the cop nearest him, who Dean figured to be about six-five or so. "It ain't you."

"We are the Last Calusa." The voice was even deeper and more resonant this time—like James Earl Jones with a bullhorn. "You have been chosen for the sacrifice. We are dead, and we are forgotten, but we are not lost. After the sacrifice, there will be vengeance, for none may trifle with the Calusa and live."

"Let's test that theory," Dean said, raising his shotgun. "I'm in the mood to trifle."

"Fine with me," Sam said, doing likewise.

Both brothers fired. The reports of their shotguns echoed into the night.

The Last Calusa was unaffected.

However, their action seemed to break the ice, as all the cops present started unloading their own nine-millimeters into the Last Calusa—with the exception of Montrose, who probably was the only one to figure out that, if two rock-salt shotgun blasts didn't do it, bullets weren't going to.

"We are *still* not impressed." The Last Calusa held up one hand, which started to glow.

Sam began, "Dean, maybe we c—"

Whirling around as his brother cut himself off in midsentence, Dean saw that Sam suddenly wasn't moving. He wasn't breathing, wasn't blinking, nothing.

Neither were any of the cops or techs.

Behind him, Montrose said, "What the hell's this?"

"The sacrifices will be prepared." The Last Calusa raised his other hand.

Dean felt as if a hand had grabbed him by the chest. Next thing he knew, he and Montrose were both flying backward, landing on the pavement of South Street near the Impala with a bone-jarring thud. His father's combat training combined with a lifetime of being thrown around by spirits and demons had taught Dean how to land properly in such an event, so he was pretty much unbruised when he clambered to his feet.

Montrose wasn't so lucky. He lay on the street, gripping his arm and wincing in pain.

Sam and the rest of the people were walking zombielike into the construction site, walking under the tarp that covered the foundation.

Dean ran toward them. "Sam!"

Even though there was nothing on the street, Dean crashed into what felt like a brick wall. He felt blood stream out of his nose from the impact.

Stumbling back a step and wiping the blood off

his upper lip, Dean reached out more carefully. He felt something solid and impenetrable, even though there was just empty air in front of him.

Great, some kind of wards.

Dean saw a bright light from behind him out of the corner of his eye, and he heard a low hum. Turning around, he saw that the Impala had started back up and its lights had gone on. The cop cars, though—which were inside the Last Calusa's little bubble—were still dead. So was the streetlight.

"Well. This sucks." He walked over to Montrose and helped him to his feet. "You okay?"

"Not especially. A whole bunch of my close friends and colleagues just got dragged into a construction site by a crazed spirit. And my arm hurts."

Before Dean could respond, his phone rang. His instinct was to let the person eat voice mail, but it might've been Bobby.

Sure enough, Bobby's name was on the display when he pulled it from his pocket, and he flipped the phone open. "Bobby, *please* tell me you've got good news."

"I do, yeah, but also bad. I know what the Last Calusa's supposed to do, but I don't know how to stop it. He takes power from living beings, draining their life. Then, at sunset, he makes a certain number of sacrifices in order to bring about his vengeance—and Dean? It's only *white* sacrifices."

Dean winced. "Okay, well, we're a step ahead of you there. Our big bad injun just put a whammy on Sam and a bunch of cops. He left one cop out of it, but he's a Seminole."

"Makes sense," Bobby said.

"Yeah, but why Sam and not me?"

Bobby hesitated. "Because you've already *been* sacrificed, Dean."

"Say what?"

"Your life already belongs to that demon you made the deal with." Bobby's temper was, Dean could tell, raging, and he was barely keeping it under control. Dean had known Bobby for most of his life, and he'd never seen the man as angry as he was when Dean told him what he'd done to save Sam's life. "The Last Calusa can't sacrifice you 'cause the sacrifice wouldn't have any power."

"Great."

"Look, I'm at the Sioux Falls airport right now—got a flight to Key West that's takin 'off in an hour or so. With the layover in Atlanta, I should be there by ten tomorrow morning. That still gives us a few hours to think'a something. Can tell you one thing, salting and burning won't cut it. We'd have to do every single set of bones of every single Calusa who ever lived, and we don't know where most of them *are*."

"Yeah, the bones here were a big surprise to everyone." Dean gritted his teeth. "I'll start digging

through Dad's journal, see if he's got anything—
maybe use Sam's laptop."

"I'll call when the flight lands," Bobby said.
"You can pick me up."

"'K."

"Dean?"

"Yeah, Bobby?"

"We'll get him back."

"Yeah." Dean closed the phone and pocketed it.

"Tough break there, kiddo."

Dean whirled around, raising the shotgun. The
voice was Montrose's, but the tone wasn't at all the
laid-back deep drawl of the cop.

Montrose—or, rather, "Fedra"—grinned widely.
"Now now, Deano, you don't want to hurt poor
Officer Montrose here, do you? And he's the only
one you would hurt with that pigsticker of yours."

While Fedra was talking with Montrose's mouth,
Dean was reaching around to the weapon he had
in the waistband of his pants. "Maybe, but this
one might do some damage," he said, lowering the
shotgun and raising the Colt.

"And, again, we're back to poor Officer Montrose. Are you *really* prepared to kill a fine, up-
standing officer of the law, a man with a wife and
four kids, just because you don't like me?"

"Montrose took an oath to serve and protect
and put his life on the line to protect people from
criminals. You've killed four people that I *know*

about, and probably a bunch more. So I'm actually pretty much okay with it." Dean hoped that his bravado was convincing because the truth was, he didn't particularly want to kill Montrose. Dean was more than happy to take someone down for the greater good, and had done so more than once. Besides, once someone was possessed by a demon, their lives were all but over. The real Fedregotti couple was evidence of that.

But that was only after long-term possession. Montrose had only been taken over for half a minute. Dean wasn't sure he could just kill someone like that. Or, rather, he knew he *could*, but didn't think he *wanted* to in this case.

Jesus, I really am *becoming the whiny emo bitch. Nothing like looking down your own personal mortality barrel to make you think about other people kicking it, I guess.*

If Dean hadn't already met Montrose, he wouldn't have known that he was possessed, since the demon hadn't done the black-eye thing. Dean still recalled when they had the yellow-eyed bastard's daughter trapped in Bobby's place, and Bobby told them that she was a regular human who was possessed. "Can't you *tell*?" Bobby had asked, and he sounded horrified that the answer was obviously "no." The method for doing so was one of a legion of things that Dad had never shared with his sons, and Dean still didn't have the trick of it down.

The demon was still talking. "Besides, I think now maybe you might want to listen to my offer."

Dean smirked. "I'd say go to hell, but—"

"Look, Dean, we both want the same thing." Montrose started to move forward toward Dean.

Clicking off the Colt's safety, Dean said, "Stay right there. You wanna talk, I'll talk for a few, but you give me a single reason to squeeze this trigger, and you're done for." Self-defense, after all, he could justify. So, for that matter, could shooting in the leg. True, it'd likely cripple Montrose for life and end his career as a cop, but it wouldn't kill him. When the yellow-eyed bastard had possessed Dad, shooting him in the leg had gotten rid of him without killing Dad. It might work a second time.

"Fine." The demon held up Montrose's hands in a backing-off gesture. "But we do. I want revenge for what that thing did to Alberto, and you want Sam back. If we work together, we can do it."

"Just for kicks—how would we do that, exactly?"

"I can cast a spell that will channel all the spiritual energy on this island through a single vessel. It's a variation on what we've *been* doing. But I need a willing human vessel to do it."

"Gee, usually you just grab somebody off the street."

"Pay attention, Dean," the demon snapped, "I said *willing*. The Last Calusa's too damn powerful—if I'm busy fighting the will of the vessel, it won't work."

"Then it won't work, 'cause I ain't *willing* to do a damn thing with your kind."

Montrose, Dean discovered, had a really unpleasant laugh. Or maybe that was the demon's doing. Either way, the cop's head reared back, and his guffaw echoed. "What, *now* you're getting all persnickety about doing a deal with a demon? Seems to me you've been down that road before when li'l bro's life was on the line. We've already established what you are, Dean—now we're just haggling over price."

For that comment alone, Dean almost pulled the trigger. Instead, he thought about Susannah and that other girl whose death got them down here in the first place. "The last two people you did your little whammy with wound up with their throats cut."

Shrugging, the demon said, "Blood helps focus the ritual, and dead girls tell no tales of Italian tourists who roofied them and escorted them out of the bar they were in. *You*, I'm not worried about blabbing. Besides, the blood isn't *necessary*, it just helps."

"You expect me to believe that? Taking a life makes the spell more powerful. So how do I know—"

"No, *sacrificing* a life makes the spell more powerful. Why do you think the Last Calusa left you out of his little confab in there? You've already lost your life, Dean, your meat's just still wandering around for a year. I don't gain anything by killing you." Another grin. "Well, nothing beyond the entertainment value." The grin fell. "But it won't help the spell any."

Dean only believed what the demon was saying because Bobby had told him the same thing. But he still didn't like the idea in the least.

"Tell you what, Dean," the demon said, "I still need to get myself a little R&R before I do this, and you'll want to consult with your South Dakota pal, and nothing's gonna happen until tomorrow at 5:43 P.M. when the sun goes down *anyhow,* so why don't I just leave the offer on the table? I'll meet you and your buddy boy Bobby at the Southernmost Point at, say, five?"

The demon didn't wait for a response, as Montrose's head reared back again, his mouth levered open, and black smoke streamed out into the night sky.

After the smoke disappeared over the ocean, Montrose coughed violently a few times. "Okay," he said in a weak voice. "That was different." He put his hand to his heart. "Always wanted to know what demonic possession felt like."

"Really?" Dean asked.

"No, not really."

Sirens started to blare in the background, and they were getting louder.

"Somebody's noticin' that the chief didn't check in," Montrose said. "You'd best vamoose. I'll cover for you. Keep me posted, all right?"

Dean made a noncommittal grunt—he had bigger concerns than keeping this guy in the loop—and got into the Impala.

I'm gonna get you out of this Sammy, I swear.

He sighed as he made a broken U-turn and sped back toward Duval. *Even if I have to work with a freakin' demon to do it.*

FIFTEEN

Sam really hated being possessed.

The last time it happened, it was for a whole week. Azazel's daughter—whom Sam and Dean still thought of as "Meg," even though that was just the name of the poor young woman she'd possessed—had crawled out of hell after Sam had exorcised her the first time at Bobby's place. She not only possessed Sam, but put a binding symbol on Sam's arm that locked her into his body. There was still a patch of tight skin where Bobby had burned off the brand, one of a network of scars, bruises, and disfigurements both brothers had gotten over the years. (Sam was still waiting for the fingernail on his right index finger to grow back after those two gods yanked it out at Christmas . . .)

Just as before, Sam was fully aware of what was going on but could do nothing about it, and just as before, it was incredibly frustrating. So far he hadn't done anything so awful as kill a man or torment a young girl, but the night was young. He needed to get free before things got any worse.

The Last Calusa had made Sam and all the cops and lab techs and the chief of police stand in a circle around the section of earth that had left the bones exposed. More dirt had been cleared away, exposing yet still more bones, which couldn't have been good.

For some reason, Dean and Officer Montrose were left out. Sam hadn't the first clue why, but he was grateful that at least his brother was still out there—assuming, of course, that the Last Calusa hadn't just killed them.

The entire time since he lost control of his own body, Sam had been struggling fiercely against it, but to no avail. Sam figured that the Last Calusa had been able to harness the life energy he drained from the construction crew to make himself stronger. Between that and the Fedregottis' spell, Sam wasn't sure how this guy was supposed to be stopped.

He tried to wiggle his finger—the one that ached from the pulled-out nail—but couldn't. "Dammit."

Only then did he realize he could talk.

Beats a poke in the eye with a sharp stick, he thought. "What're you gonna do with us?"

The Last Calusa turned to stare at him from

behind the ornate mask from where they stood inside the circle, though not actually stepping on any of the bones. "We will enact the vengeance of the Calusa."

"Which is what, exactly?"

Before the Last Calusa could speak, the chief of police said, "What're you talking to this lunatic for? I don't know what kind of game you're playing, mister, but—"

"Silence!" The Last Calusa gestured, and suddenly the chief couldn't speak, though his mouth continued to move.

"Leave him alone!" one of the cops said. "You've got no right to—"

Another gesture, and the cop was also silenced. "What of our right to survive? We were the mightiest of warriors in our time. Some came to the Calusa for protection, and they were rewarded. Others tried to take what belonged to the Calusa, and they were punished. Their bones littered the ground as testament to their foolishness in challenging us."

Now the Last Calusa paced around the circumference of the bones, staying within the circle of the possessed. "For many seasons, we thrived. Then came the outsiders with their strange clothing and odd tools. And their sickness. Illness was always a part of our lives, but the outsiders' diseases could not be cured by our priests. The outsiders were able to do what the warriors of many a tribe could not: They brought low the Calusa."

Standing in front of Sam now, the Last Calusa stared at him. Through the painted wooden mask, Sam saw eyes that seemed to change color every few seconds. The deep, hollow voice—which continued to speak a language Sam did not know, for all that he continued to understand every word—came out in a muffled echo through the wood.

"As our people died, the priests came together, knowing they needed to take action. When there were only a handful of Calusa left alive, one priest was able to bind the eye souls of the dead together so that one day they might achieve vengeance on those who destroyed us. When the time was right for us to return, we did. We steal the lives from the outsiders, as they stole the life from us with their disease. Once we have sufficient strength, all outsiders will be destroyed. *That* is the vengeance of the Calusa."

"Great," Sam muttered.

Sam noticed that the Last Calusa had a solid presence. Spirits were often more ethereal. In fact, the only thing that gave away that the Last Calusa was anything other than corporeal was that he had no *smell*. The wood the mask was made of, the paint that decorated it, the musk of the Last Calusa—Sam couldn't smell any of it. The only olfactory hit was the dirt of the ground around him and the salty tang of the ocean breeze.

That had been true of Molly as well. Her spirit was fully corporeal, and relived the same accident every year for fifteen years, and while Sam could touch her, he'd never been able to smell anything on her.

"What does this accomplish?" Sam asked. "The Calusa will still be dead. And it's been over two hundred years. None of the people who invaded your land then are around anymore. This peninsula has belonged to several different nations since then. Most of the people who live here aren't even descended from the ones who killed your people."

"It will accomplish what we were created to accomplish: vengeance. That is all that matters." The Last Calusa stepped back. "You will remain here until next the sun retreats. Then it will end."

As he spoke, the Last Calusa faded away into nothingness.

But Sam still couldn't move. He had hoped that he might be able to reason with the spirit even though he knew it to be a long shot. Vengeance spirits, though, were like computers: They could only do what they were programmed to do and couldn't move beyond that. Garbage in, garbage out.

"What the *hell* is going *on* here?" the chief of police asked. "This is insane, how can—?"

"Chief," one of the cops said, "with all due respect, shut the hell up. You—kid."

Sam realized that the cop was talking to him. "Yeah?"

"I'm guessing you're one of the hunters on the island that Van told us about?"

The chief was getting apoplectic. "Hunters? What the hell does some jackass shooting deer have to do with—"

"Yes, my brother and I met Officer Montrose last night. My name's Sam Winchester."

"You know how to stop this thing, Winchester?" another cop asked.

Hedging his bets, Sam said, "There are lots of ways to destroy a spirit."

"Don't play mind games, son," a third cop said, "we do this for a living. Right present, I'd prefer an honest answer to fake reassurances."

"Me, too."

"Yeah."

The chief, though, yelled, "What are you people *talking* about?"

Since his own people were ignoring him, Sam felt comfortable disregarding the chief as well. "I'm not sure. A spirit like this, there's two ways to get rid of it. One works on most every spirit: You salt and burn its physical remains."

"How come you said 'most every'?" the first cop asked.

"Well, sometimes the remains are cremated or otherwise destroyed. And—" He hesitated. "And sometimes the spirit's too powerful for that to work."

Silence descended upon the site for a moment. Then the chief burst out: "You people are *insane*! Spirits? This is nonsense!"

"You been livin' on Key West *how* long, boss?" another cop asked.

"I don't believe in ghosts," the chief said archly.

"What'd you think that was, Chief, a special effect? And hey, how come you ain't movin' right now?"

The chief started muttering. "Crazy, just—just *crazy*."

A lab tech spoke over the chief. "You said there were two ways to get rid of it, Mr. Winchester. You implied the first method won't work here."

"It won't," Sam said. "This spirit is the embodiment of the entire tribe. We'd never be able to track all the remains down."

"Fine," the lab tech said. "What's the other?"

"The Last Calusa is a vengeance spirit. It's here for a particular purpose. Some spirits are here to warn somebody about something, or let people know who really killed them, that kind of thing. Once they've fulfilled that purpose, they move on."

"So once this guy does what he's supposed to do, he'll go away?" a cop asked.

"Yeah."

"Great," another cop said, "so all we gotta do to get rid of this guy is wait for him to wipe the entire human race. Swell."

"Not all of us," Sam said. "He said all 'outsiders' would die. And you notice he didn't drag Officer Montrose in here. My guess is that sacrificing us will give him the power he needs to wipe out all non-Indian people. Or maybe he'll spare the members of tribes he considers friendly to the Calusa. "

"This is insane," the chief said.

"I'm with the chief," one of the cops said. "He's just gonna kill us 'cause his people got sick? I mean, he said it himself, it was disease that wiped 'em out! That's not even anybody's fault!"

"I didn't see *you* trying to explain that to him," another lab tech said.

"It was pretty obvious that listenin' to reason wasn't high on this guy's list."

The cops continued to argue. Sam tuned it out, trying to focus inward. Maybe, if he concentrated hard enough, he could break free of the Last Calusa's imprisonment.

Several moments of concentration later—though Sam wasn't sure how long, since he couldn't move his arm to see what time it was—and he had no luck.

So he concentrated some more. *I've got until a quarter to six or so tomorrow, and it's not like I have anything better to do . . .*

SIXTEEN

Dean sat not-very-patiently on the hood of the Impala, currently parked on Route 1A near the Key West International Airport. *Which*, Dean thought, *is a pretty hifalutin name for a shack with a runway*. Still, they had flights to various foreign countries—many of which were closer to Key West than the island was to the Florida state capital—so Dean supposed it made sense.

Bobby had said his flight would be in around ten. Dean supposed he could have gone inside and checked, but that would've required setting foot in an airport, which Dean had no interest in doing. That would put him in dangerous proximity to the planes. It was bad enough the damn things kept flying overhead and making all that noise as they came crashing—okay, *landing*—to the ground.

He didn't see how Bobby could even consider traveling that way. Of course, it made more sense right now, since they only had until sunset tonight. Sam had whined any number of times about how ridiculous it was that they had to drive everywhere. And even Dean had to admit that being grounded limited them. But air travel was expensive, as was storing the Impala (though Bobby would let them keep it at his place for free). More important, how the hell were they supposed to transport their weaponry? Dean had plenty of faith in his and his brother's ability to forge documentation, but it was a lot easier to fool a grieving widow or an over-worked hospital nurse than airport security.

Sammy . . .

Dean shook his head—then jumped out of his skin as he heard another plane take off. *Goddam-mit.*

Route 1A ran along the southeast coast of the island, and in this spot it was the beach and the ocean on one side and the airport on the other. If he faced one way, he could see the planes, and he broke out in a cold sweat. If he faced the ocean—which had the added advantage of affording him a view of the women on the beach—he was caught off guard by the sounds of the planes, and it scared the crap out of him.

If Dean *had* to have a phobia, he supposed fear of flying was as good a one as any to have in his line of work. Beat the hell out of claustrophobia or a fear of loud noises. Dean had no problem with fear, as long as it stayed healthy. Healthy fear kept you alive. Crippling, mind-numbing, paralyzing, sweat-inducing fear, though, that sucked. And messed with the job.

The job was all Dean had. Yes, he had Sam, too, but Sammy was intricately tied up *with* the job.

He pounded the hood of the Impala and hopped off it, starting to pace on the sidewalk. *Times like this, I wish I smoked. This'd be a great time for a cigarette.* Not that it would help matters, and they had enough problems keeping up with rising gas prices, much less adding a habit that cost five bucks a pack.

But that was the job. Cheap motels, cheap coffee, cheap beer, cheap food that was probably hardening his arteries by the second, all of it a testament to getting what you paid for.

My health don't matter, though. Why should I worry about a heart attack or lung cancer when I'm fifty when I ain't even gonna see my thirtieth birthday?

A tinny rendition of Eric Clapton's guitar riff for "Crossroads" sounded from Dean's pocket. Taking out his cell phone, he saw that it was Bobby. *Guess one of those planes was his.* "Yeah, Bobby?"

"Plane's landed."

"Okay—I'm right down the street. See you in a few."

About twenty minutes later, Dean was waiting at the car pickup area near the terminal when Bobby finally emerged, holding a small carry-on bag. "I also had some stuff shipped overnight to the Naylor House. It show up yet?"

"Dunno," Dean said. "I haven't been there in a while." He assumed that Bobby had sent along things you couldn't really bring on a plane.

Bobby threw his bag into the backseat, then stared at Dean through the passenger-side window. "You okay? The bags under your eyes have bags under their eyes."

Dean shook his head. "I was up all night digging through Dad's journal. Didn't find jack about the Last Calusa or about demon rituals that destroy powerful spirits. After that, I got sick of sitting in the damn room, so I went driving up and down the keys for a while."

Bobby opened the door and climbed into the passenger seat. "After dealing with John's thought processes, I'd need a long drive myself. C'mon, let's figure out what's goin' on."

Dean yanked on the seat belt. Something about having Bobby in the car made him want to play it safe. He didn't always bother with it, though lately he'd been putting it on when Sam whined about it, just to avoid yet another argument. He and Sam had been bickering *way* too much lately as it was. Besides, with both of them on the federal radar, it'd be downright embarrassing to be nailed at a traffic stop for piddly crap like a seat belt and get tossed back into the waiting arms of Special Agent Henriksen.

For Bobby, though, Dean buckled up on instinct. Out of respect, if nothing else.

It had been a very frustrating night. Pulling an all-nighter was fine if you actually *got* something out of it, but all Dean had done was read through the overstuffed leather-bound notebook that was all he had left of his and Sam's father. In the years since the yellow-eyed bastard killed their mother, John had dedicated himself to being a hunter, and all that time he took copious notes.

What they weren't, though, were organized notes. Aside from sticking the stuff that was phony in the back, Dad didn't keep his notes in anything like order. Sammy had been making noise about putting the whole thing into a database or something on his laptop, but he hadn't actually had time to do so, what with them being so busy doing their jobs and all.

So Dean spent the entire night squinting over Dad's weird handwriting and upside-down margin notes and total lack of organizational skills, all to find out that this was something he never encountered in two decades of hunting. Or if he did, he didn't bother writing it down.

Thanks, Dad. Big help, like always.

To make matters worse, Captain Naylor wasn't

doing so hot at keeping his promise to leave Dean alone, as he kept showing up in the room to ask how things were proceeding. He also expressed displeasure at what the Fedregottis did to him, at great length.

Finally, Dean got fed up and left.

"You get my message?" Dean asked as he headed back westward toward Old Town.

"Yeah, got the voice mail when we stopped over in Atlanta. And I don't like it."

"Me either, but unless you got a better idea . . ."

"*Anything's* a better idea than workin' with a demon, Dean."

"Really?" Dean said snidely. "So that *wasn't* a demon who helped you rebuild the Colt, that was just some blond chick with *really* black eyes, right?"

Bobby said nothing.

"Look," Dean went on, "you said that Tonto can't use me because my life's already been sacrificed. Well, I *made* that sacrifice so that Sammy wouldn't die. I ain't lettin' that be for nothing, so we are doing whatever it takes to make sure he lives. If that means workin' with that bitch of a demon, then we do that."

"I don't like it, Dean."

"Excuse me, but when did *liking* ever enter the freakin' equation? This is *Sam* we're talkin' about!"

"Yeah, and you already did one stupid-ass thing to save his life, and I don't want you doin' another one without *thinkin'* about it first." Bobby pointed an accusatory finger at Dean from the passenger seat. "And don't you *dare* take that tone with me, boy. I been in this game a lot longer than you, and I know all about what you have to do when things get bad."

Bobby didn't elaborate, and Dean didn't ask, mostly because he was embarrassed. Bobby was as close to a father as Dean had anymore. Hell, in some ways, he was better than the guy who originally had the job, and he certainly didn't deserve to have Dean biting his head off. "I'm sorry, Bobby."

"It's all right," Bobby said in a quieter tone. "I shouldn'ta snapped. But you ain't the only one's been up all night."

They drove in silence for a few minutes.

"What exactly did the demon say she could do?" Bobby asked.

Turning the Impala right onto White Street, Dean said, "She said her spell could channel all the spiritual energy on Key West through a single vessel."

"And you're the single vessel?"

Dean nodded. "Has to be a willing vessel; otherwise, she's spending too much time struggling with the guy and isn't able to focus."

"Makes sense." Bobby's lips twisted in thought.

"The Last Calusa's got the strength of the entire tribe, with the added bonus of all the people he killed. The spirits on the island are already more powerful thanks to the demons' spell. Combine 'em all into one person—"

"And you got one bad-ass spirit," Dean said.

"Sonofabitch." Bobby suddenly got a faraway look in his eyes.

"Bobby?" Dean prompted as he turned left onto Eaton.

Shaking his head, Bobby said, "I'm a jackass. Shoulda realized it when I heard your voice mail. This sounds like a variation on a gestalt."

"Gesundheit."

Bobby didn't even dignify that with a reply, which Dean found disappointing. Sam, at least, he could count on for a groan of appreciation. Instead, Bobby just said, "It's a spell that combines several people into one."

"You ever seen this spell in action?"

"No." Bobby shook his head emphatically. "This is high-level stuff, the sorta thing that monks could only pull off after fifty straight years of meditation."

"Or a demon could do in her sleep."

"Yeah."

Pulling into the Naylor House's driveway, Dean said, "So basically we're fighting fire with fire. Tonto's a ghost to the power of a thousand, so we hit *him* with a ghost to the power of a thousand."

"Pretty much, yeah." Bobby climbed out of the car and opened the back to retrieve his bag.

Bodge was sitting on the front porch, Snoopy draped over her lap, snoozing. "Heya Deany-baby! You got a package. Nicki's got it inside."

The salutation got Dean a look from Bobby, which Dean ignored with only a little more effort than it took to ignore similar looks from Sam. "Thanks, Bodge! This is our friend Bobby."

"Pleased to meet you, Bob. I'd get up, but, uh—" She pointed at the sleeping sheepdog.

Bobby smiled. "Got a pooch of my own. If he ain't up and runnin' over to meet new people, means he's out like a light."

"Yeah." Bodge laughed. "There's some breakfast left in back if you guys want."

"Thanks," Dean said as he hopped up onto the porch. He paused to give Snoopy a scritch. The dog raised his furry head for a brief second, then flopped back down onto Bodge's thigh.

Inside, Nicki was sitting at the front desk, and Dean introduced Bobby to her as he signed for the package, then they took the big box and went out into the back. The table had two pitchers of coffee, several bowls filled with cut fruit, a loaf of bread next to a toaster, a butter dish, several jars of jam, and a few boxes of cereal.

"They only do the fancy breakfast from six to nine," Dean said dolefully. Of course, he could have had it this morning, but he had been up around Key Largo at that point.

"This'll do." Bobby poured himself some coffee and put two slices of bread in the toaster.

After they'd stocked up on fruit, toast, and coffee, they retired to Dean's room.

Captain Naylor was waiting for them, predictably. "I see you've brought assistance thanks to your brother's capture. Good morning, sir. I am Captain Terrence Naylor, and I'm a prisoner of this blasted house."

Nonplussed, Bobby said, "Er, Bobby Singer. Friend'a Dean and Sam's."

"Mr. Winchester and I have an arrangement," Naylor said.

"Yeah," Dean said through gritted teeth, "that you'd *leave me alone*, and I'd salt and burn your bones when this was all over. You ain't doin' so hot on your end."

Sounding wholly unapologetic, Naylor said, "My apologies, but my already-nightmarish existence has grown far worse."

"My heart bleeds."

"Actually," Bobby said, "we're gonna need your help to get this done. You and all the spirits on the island."

"And how's that, Mr. Singer?"

Quickly, Bobby explained what he assumed the spell to be. "If there's anything you can do to smooth matters over with the other spirits, it might help."

"I doubt I have that sort of influence over my fellow deceased—however, in the interests of fulfilling my side of our arrangement, I will endeavor to do so."

With that, he faded away.

Dean fixed Bobby with a dubious expression. "You really think Captain Ahab there can talk the other spirits into cooperating?"

Bobby shrugged. "Got nothin' to lose by tryin'. Maybe the horse'll talk."

"Sorry?" Dean asked in confusion. It was a sad commentary on Dean's life that it was perfectly possible that Bobby really *meant* an actual talking horse.

"Story my uncle used to tell," Bobby said after sipping his coffee. "Guy's being condemned to death. He's brought before the king, and the king asks if he has any last words. Guy says, 'Your majesty, gimme a year, and I can teach your horse how to talk.' The king thinks this sounds good, so he stays the guy's execution for a year and tells him to go to the stables and teach his horse to talk. The guy's friend goes up to him, and says, 'What're you, nuts? You can't teach a horse to talk, nobody can!' The guy says, 'Look, I've got a year. Maybe I'll die. Maybe the king'll die. And hey—maybe the horse'll talk.'"

Dean just stared at Bobby for a second. Then he reached into his pocket to pull out a knife. "Here's to talking horses."

Slicing open Bobby's box, he saw your basic hunter's toolkit, including a mess of holy water, a few charms, and some weaponry, of both the firearm and bladed variety.

"If this spell works the way I think it does," Bobby said, "the demon'll possess someone and cast the spell on you."

"Why not just channel it through the person she's possessing?"

"If she said it wouldn't be powerful enough if she had to fight the will of the vessel, then she probably would have the same problem if she tried to channel it through her own vessel."

Dean sighed. "Good thing we got those charms to keep us from getting possessed." Bobby had given Dean and Sam the charms after Meg took over Sammy, and since then, both brothers had gotten the charm tattooed on their chests, with the charms themselves stored in the Impala in reserve.

"Yeah." Bobby scratched his beard. "Let's hope it works."

That brought Dean up short. "You don't know if the charms will work?"

"Nothing's sure in this world, Dean. You of all people should know that by now. And this demon's proven to be pretty tricky. I'm not assumin' anything."

"Can't say as I blame you."

"Good. Now here's what I think we should do . . ."

Bobby Singer had led a quiet, normal life for a long time. Married, owned his own business, had some money in the bank, was well respected in the community. He was happy as could be, living the American Dream.

Then something happened to his wife. At the time, he didn't know what it was, but in the end, he was forced to kill her before she killed anyone else. He stabbed her repeatedly—once didn't do it—and eventually she died, weird black smoke flowing from her mouth.

From that moment forward, Bobby was consumed with anguish, not as much by the fact that he killed his wife, but because *he didn't know what happened to her.* He'd never been particularly book-smart. Sure, he knew his way around a motor vehicle, and he did okay in school, neither a poor student nor one who excelled.

But after he was forced to kill his own wife to stop whatever it was that had taken her over, Bobby swore he would never live in such ignorance again. He set out to learn everything he could. The once-pristine house attached to the salvage yard in which he had lived in wedded bliss quickly became covered in shelves full of books, scrolls, maps, and more. Never again would someone die because Bobby Singer didn't know what was happening.

The guilt intensified when Bobby realized that he could have saved her with a simple Latin incantation—an exorcism, like they did in the movie. That knowledge nearly destroyed him, but he soldiered on, devouring every text he could get his hands on so he would know everything about the shadowy world of magic and deviltry.

Before long, he gained a reputation in the community of hunters, those people who lived under the radar and tracked down the things that went bump in the night. He was the go-to guy if you needed lore or information. (Also if you needed your car fixed. He still had a business to run, after all . . .) Among hunters it was often said that if Bobby didn't know it, it wasn't worth knowing.

That just made the guilt even worse.

Of all the friends he'd made over the years, though, no one frustrated him quite as much as John Winchester. Moody and ornery, unwilling to share information, yet irritable when you didn't give him exactly what *he* wanted, John had come to Bobby a lot in the early days when he was just starting out.

The last time Bobby saw John alive, he came within a hairsbreadth of unloading his shotgun into John's gut. Truth of the matter was, that day only took so long to come because of Sam and Dean. Bobby loved those boys like they were his own, and it was always a source of pride to him that they called him "Uncle Bobby" when they were younger.

Everything Bobby had learned over the years had told him that demons were not to be messed with. You exorcised them and moved on. You didn't talk to them, you didn't do deals with them, you didn't give them a single chance, because the microsecond you let your guard down, they'd nail you. That was why he'd been so livid when Dean informed him of the deal he'd made with the cross-roads demon to save Sam's life.

So what the hell am I doing helping Dean work with another *demon? What was I doing asking Ruby's help to rebuild the Colt?*

Things were changing, that was for damn sure. The demons were all over the place since the Dev-il's Gate opened, and as far as he could see, a lot of them were gearing up for a war. As the only sur-vivor of Azazel's chosen ones, there was a better-than-even chance that Sam was a part of it.

For better or worse, that meant Dean and Bobby were part of it, too. They just had to hope they'd be on the winning side.

He and Dean had driven in the Impala to the construction site—or as close as they could get.

The wards were, of course, still there. A massive cordon had been set up beyond them, including local cops, county cops, state cops, and the U.S. Navy.

After going on a quick reconnaissance, Dean came back to the car. "Saw our guy Montrose. He says they've been tryin' to get through all day, but no luck."

"Not surprising. Doubt there's any force on Earth—or elsewhere—that could get through."

Dean climbed back behind the steering wheel. "Montrose said he could see inside. Sammy, the cops, and the lab techs're all standing in a circle around the bones. They ain't moved since last night."

"Didja try the dust?"

Nodding, Dean said, "Yeah. It stuck to the wards like you said it would, so we'll be able to see 'em."

Bobby looked at his watch. "Almost five. Time to meet our demon."

"Yeah." Dean slammed the steering wheel as hard as he could and screamed incoherently, then let loose with an impressive display of profanity, pounding the steering wheel the whole time.

A few seconds after he started, Dean stopped, turned the key, and calmly turned the car around. Bobby wasn't sure if it was a good thing or not that Dean felt comfortable enough with Bobby to let out his frustration like that. He knew for damn sure that Dean would *never* in a million years lose his cool like that in front of Sam.

The Southernmost Point was a black, red, and yellow piece of concrete shaped to look like a boat's buoy. It sat in the corner of a plaza at the intersections of Whitehead and South Streets, which was the farthest south Key West got—and was only two blocks from the construction site. At five in the afternoon, Bobby expected to see more tourists taking pictures of themselves with the buoy.

But the only person present was an attractive young brunette. She was short, curvy, and wearing only a light green bathing-suit top, denim cutoffs, and light green mesh sandals.

She was also holding a thin digital camera, and as Dean and Bobby approached, she practically bounced. "Ooh! Excuse me, can one of you take a picture of me next to the buoy? I totally need it for my Facebook page."

Dean put on one of his more blinding smiles. "Be happy to, but after that, I'm afraid I'm gonna have to ask you to head off. We've got a meeting here, and we really don't want any tourists around."

"Really? You guys are, like, drug dealers or something? Got any good stuff?"

Bobby had had more than enough of this. The only way one of the major tourist attractions on the island would be this empty at this time of day in good weather was if the one person present had used her demonic abilities to send away everyone else. "Cut the crap, lady. You *are* our meeting, so let's get on with it."

"Nice touch," Dean added. "What, you thought it'd be easier to talk me into it if you took over a hot chick?"

The young woman's eyes went black. "Yes, actually."

Snorting, Bobby said, "That's pretty transparent, even by demon standards."

"Transparent ploy for a transparent hunter," the woman said. "Dean's pretty easy to read. The hard part was narrowing it down to one particular busty bikini-clad babe. Besides, I figured Dean was less likely to use his little toy gun on me if it meant killing poor, innocent little Kat. Nice girl, goes to Augustana College—that's near your little car graveyard in South Dakota, isn't it, Singer? She hasn't decided on a major yet, and she's spending a couple weeks in the Keys before the semester starts."

"There's other ways to get rid of you," Dean said tightly.

"You never really struck me as the Latin-chanting type, Dean."

"Dean ain't the only one here," Bobby said. "Now we'll work with you on this, 'cause believe it or not, you're the lesser of two evils right now.

But I will be carrying the Colt, and I know every exorcism ritual you can think of. Trust me when I say that if I see a single thing goin' hinky, I will end you—even if it means ending Kat, too. We understand each other?"

The demon smiled with the pouty lips of the girl she'd possessed. "Clear as mud, boys. Let's get to work, shall we? Time's a-wastin', and we've got work to do."

Bobby had a sinking feeling in his gut that before this night was over, Kat was going to wind up dead, too.

SEVENTEEN

Sam had fought many battles over the years, earned many victories. He had defeated gods and demons, devils and spirits, imps and impossible things.

But just at the moment, managing to wiggle his left thumb was the sweetest victory he could imagine. Probably because he'd been trying for the better part of a day.

The sun shining through the tarp that covered the site was the only way for Sam and his fellow prisoners to judge the passage of time—which meant it had been a particularly long and frustrating night, as subjective time tended to draw out when you didn't have access to a timepiece. Everyone was relieved when the sky started to brighten with the sunrise.

Sam had suggested that everyone try to get some sleep in the night so they'd be rested when the Last Calusa came back, but that only met with mild success. Sam had slept in far more bizarre places and positions than standing upright and immobile in a construction site—plus, being forced into such a position wasn't exactly a novel experience. His companions could not say the same on either front. They were sufficiently freaked and frustrated that sleep was hard to come by.

By sunrise, they had devolved into banter and gossip. Soon, Sam knew far more than he ever needed to know about the internal politics of the KWPD.

Unable to contribute, Sam continued to turn his mind inward. It was just a question of overcoming the paralysis. It was imposed by the will of the Last Calusa. True, that spirit had the collective power of thousands, maybe millions of once-living souls, along with those, both human and demon, that the Last Calusa had killed since being activated. But it also had to hold all the people in the site immobile, plus do whatever it needed to do to prepare for the sacrifice ceremony at sunset.

And Sam Winchester could be a damn stubborn ass when he put his mind to it. *Just ask my Dad when I insisted I go to Stanford. Or my brother when I refused to accept that he's gonna die.*

So he focused. And concentrated. And pushed. And grimaced. And agonized. And pushed some more. And after many many hours of that, he finally was able to wiggle his right thumb.

One down, the rest of the body to go.

Sam opened his eyes. He was grateful that he even could. Because the Last Calusa needed them alive, he allowed them to continue to breathe. Sam supposed that he allowed them to blink so their vision would be clear at the appointed time, and they could see the end of the world as they knew it.

As for being able to speak . . . In Sam's experience, if somebody with malicious intent kept your mouth free, nine times out of ten it was because they wanted to hear you scream.

The cops and lab techs were apparently discussing a case. Sam figured that was a good way to avoid thinking about the insane situation they were in: Focus on the quotidian.

"The problem was," one was saying, "they were stupid. They shouldn't let stupid people dive."

"If we stopped people bein' stupid," another cop said, "we'd never get any *real* work done."

"Amen."

"Besides," said one of the lab techs, "weren't those guys from New Jersey? What the hell do they know about scuba diving in *New Jersey*? They didn't even have a dive reel, for Christ's sake."

"Actually, the Jersey divers I've met have been totally hard-core. Best divers I've ever seen. Till these jokers, anyhow."

"You ask me, that's natural selection at work."

While they babbled on, Sam continued to wiggle

his thumb, hoping for a cascade effect on the rest of his hand. Once, Sam had had mental powers that enabled him to see future events. On one particular occasion, he'd even managed a brief burst of telekinesis. It was, he later learned, the first step toward the full psychic powers that would enable him to lead Azazel's demon army.

Since Dean shot Azazel with the Colt, there hadn't been any sign of those psychic abilities. For the first time, Sam came close to regretting that. Not that he particularly wanted those demonic abilities to return, but he didn't want most of the human race to be wiped out, either.

The sun was no longer shining directly on the tarp, which meant that Sam was running out of time. He hoped that Dean was working an angle of his own. Hell, he hoped that Dean was still alive. He'd had all night to think about it, and it was perfectly possible that Dean wasn't included because the Last Calusa only needed a specific number of white lives to sacrifice, and since Dean was the "extra," the Last Calusa just killed him.

Hope that's not true, but I have to proceed as if it is. So he kept trying to move his whole hand.

Dean drove as fast as he could on South Street the two blocks to the construction site. He wanted to have the Impala as close to ground zero as possible. But the demon insisted on riding in the back.

Dean wanted to make her walk the two blocks, but she insisted. "What, you're willing to do a deal with me, but not willing to let me sit in your pwecious widdle car?" she had asked.

"Pretty much, yeah."

"Dean," Bobby had said.

"Fine, whatever."

He practically jumped out of the car as he parked it just outside the wards and threw open the back door. Jerking his thumb, he said, "Out!"

"Yes, Daddy," the demon said in a pouty tone.

Dean practically snarled. Kat was exactly the kind of girl Dean would be all over if he met her in a Duval Street bar, but knowing that "Fedra" was in there made him want to whip out the Colt and take a shot.

Speaking of which, he pulled it out of his waistband and handed it to Bobby.

Bobby took it with a nod, then said, "I take it the empty street's your doing, little lady?"

"Good guess," the demon said with a sweet smile. "Can't really do my best work with that big an audience, y'know? And before you both get your panties in a bunch, I just made them forget that anything was happening here and leave the site. It's a temporary thing—by morning, they'll be back to normal. But by then, one way or another, it won't matter."

"My panties weren't in a bunch, thanks," Dean

said, pulling out the bag of dust Bobby had given him. He pulled out a deep handful and tossed it forward on the street. It hovered in midair in a splatter pattern, as if he'd tossed against a sticky brick wall.

"Neither were mine." The demon's smile turned wicked. "But then, this young woman isn't wearing any."

Dean closed his eyes, took a breath, quickly banished the mental image, then looked around again. "The wards moved. When I crashed into them last night, they were about even with that fire hydrant." Dean pointed at the hydrant in question, which was now behind where the dust had collected.

"Prob'ly from our cop and military buddies. They ain't happy 'less they're shootin' at somethin'," Bobby said, "and the wards must be designed to expand at any sign of serious resistance."

The demon rolled Kat's eyes. "Brilliant deduction, Watson. Some of us already knew that. Can we get on with this, please? It's already ten after five, and we have a lot of prep work to do. Singer, would you be *ever* so kind as to draw a pentagram on the pavement? And make sure it's pointing the *right* way."

"You mean the wrong way, don'tcha?" Bobby asked with a snide smile.

"Bite me, Redneck Boy, you want this to work or not? Demonic magic means reverse pentagram."

"Yeah, yeah." Bobby took a stick of chalk out of his pocket and started drawing.

"You need me to do anything?" Dean asked.

The demon pulled a knife out of her pocket and held it with her left hand. "Just stand there and look cute." Then she sliced open her right palm with the blade.

It happened so fast, Dean barely registered that it had happened when it was all over. He lunged forward and grabbed her left wrist. "What the hell're you—?"

"*Will* you take a chill pill already?"

She reached up and ran her palm down Dean's chin. He felt the slickness of Kat's blood and instinctively moved to wipe it off.

Breaking Dean's grip with appalling ease, the demon then grabbed *his* wrist. "The blood binds us together for the spell. Let me say it again in closed-captioning for the hearing-impaired—do you want this to work or not?"

"I ain't gonna let you harm that girl."

Kat's face grew hard, and her eyes went black. "Grow up, Dean. You wanna make an omelette, some eggs are gonna get cracked. I need this meat puppet alive to do this anyhow, and all I sliced open was her palm—not the veins in the wrist or the carotid or the femoral. So get over your big self and *let me do this*."

Through gritted teeth, Dean said, "Fine."

"Good." The demon smiled, her eyes going back to their usual blue, and wiped her palm on Dean's other cheek.

Feeling fully soiled, Dean asked, "Now what?"

"Prepare yourself. The spirits of a lot of very unhappy dead people are going to get slammed into your consciousness all at once. You've got to stay focused. Pick something—a happy memory, a thought, a song you like, a pretty girl you banged, whatever—and focus on that to the exclusion of all else. That should ground you. I need you aware, which means you've got to beat down the other voices that are gonna be in your head." The demon moved closer to him. Dean could smell the chlorine from the pool that Kat had apparently used within the last few hours. "You sure you're up for this?"

"Wouldn't have said yes if I wasn't, bitch. Get on with it."

She chuckled. "That's my boy."

"Not hardly."

Bobby stood upright. "Pentagram's done."

The demon looked down at the pavement. "Wow."

"What?" Bobby asked, sounding confused.

"I've never seen a freehand pentagram drawn so neatly."

Dean blew out a laugh. *Typical Bobby.*

The demon then closed Kat's eyes and started

breathing more slowly. She folded her legs under her in a lotus position. Belatedly, Dean realized that she hadn't lowered herself to the street but picked her legs up off the ground and was now floating over the reverse pentagram.

She opened her eyes, and they'd gone all black again.

Bobby stood to the side and hefted the Colt. "Don't think my incredibly neat freehand pentagram's gonna protect you from this, little lady."

"Wouldn't dream of it, Bobby-boy. Look, we don't trust each other. I get that. We'll do this, wipe out the Last Calusa, save humanity, avenge Alberto, then I'll go back to being the Legion of Doom to your Super Friends, 'k?"

"Sounds good to me." Dean then turned his back on the demon and Bobby, and closed his eyes, slowing his breathing down. Dad had sent Dean to a martial-arts school when he was a kid, but he'd never taken to it. It didn't help that they moved around so much that he kept having to start over as a beginner at every new dojo, but Dean also wasn't very good at the whole discipline thing. He was more of a brawler.

So Dad had trained Dean himself, teaching his son what the Marines had taught him. But there were a few elements of Asian martial arts that had been part of that, and one was controlling your breathing. Dean put his hands out straight in front of him, pulled them in toward his chest as he inhaled for six heartbeats, held his breath for three heartbeats, then lowered his hands toward his hips while exhaling for six more heartbeats.

He repeated this a few more times, while taking the demon's advice about finding something to focus on. But it wasn't a happy memory (not enough of those), a song he liked (though he briefly considered "Kashmir"), or a sexual encounter (too many of those).

No, he focused on the one thing that he knew would keep him grounded the way the demon said he'd need to be.

"Take your brother outside as fast as you can— don't look back. Now, Dean, go!"

Sam's not dying. Not on my watch. You protect your family no matter what.

I'm coming for you, Sammy. Just hold tight.

And don't look back.

He opened his eyes. Behind him, he could hear Kat's voice muttering an incantation in a language he didn't recognize. It wasn't Latin, certainly. Since it *was* demon magic, it was probably some language that was even more dead than Latin.

The chanting stopped.

Dean screamed.

EIGHTEEN

. . . he had been saying "today is the day" for years now. Hunting for treasure under the reef-laden seas of south Florida had been a passion of his and his family's since the 1950s. But when he learned of the *Nuestra Señora de Atocha* in 1968—a Spanish sailing vessel that was written up as one of the richest shipwrecks ever lost—finding it became his life's work. It had been lost in the Florida Keys, specifically near Key West.

He and his wife and children all moved to Key West, and they continued to seek the great treasure. The search for the Mother Lode had literally taken decades, and claimed the life of his oldest son.

But still they soldiered on. Still he insisted "today is the day." Financed by his years of running a dive shop, by investors who wanted a piece of the Mother Lode, and people who were willing to work for almost nothing, he kept searching, kept hoping, never once giving up.

They mocked him, they said he was a money-grubbing treasure hunter, they said he was a charlatan, they said he was a con man. But, this being Key West, mostly they just left him alone. Everyone knew about the crazy old treasure hunter and his equally crazy family. And who knew? Maybe someday he'd find it. Maybe someday, today really *would* be the day.

And then today finally came on this hot July day in 1985. It had been his youngest son, Kane, who'd found it, radioing back to Key West while he was buying new diving fins.

They'd found the Mother Lode. Over a thousand silver bars, and boxes of coins with three thousand coins in each.

Now he walked down the streets of Key West, being congratulated by total strangers on the street—who all knew him, of course, he was a Key West institution by now, never mind that most people thought him nuts—and he swelled with pride. He'd known all along that he would find the treasure.

He gave silent thanks to Dirk, tragically lost almost exactly a decade before. *I'm sorry you didn't get to see this, son.*

A tall young man with shaggy hair and hazel

eyes walked up to him and shook his hand enthusiastically. "This is a great day, isn't it?"

Sam . . .

. . . she couldn't take it anymore.

Everything had gone downhill since they left Key Largo. She had loved it down there, but Dad got a new job, and Mom insisted that they had to move to Chattanooga, even though it was the middle of the school year, and all her friends were *here*. The road trips down to Key West or up to Miami, the trips in Ellie's father's boat, volunteering to help out at the birding and wildlife festival on Marathon Key, and so much more.

She had fought Mom and Dad every step of the way, throwing tantrums and crying and saying that there was no way this could possibly work. "I'll be miserable!" "It'll suck!" "Everyone there'll hate me!" That last was heartfelt, as she recalled the way everyone treated kids who transferred in midsemester: They were just *tortured*.

But nobody listened to her. Nobody ever did. So off they all went to Chattanooga, and sure enough, all the kids tormented her. "Noob!" "Ain't in Florida no more!" "Why don't you come to our hangout? You mean you don't *know* where it is? Why not?"

Then she made the mistake of trying to fit in by

getting drunk with the cool kids. Except the cool kids had roofies.

No one believed the rape story. It didn't help that she could barely remember what happened, only vague recollections of several boys pulling down their pants and a constant ache between her legs that had yet to go away.

Mom wanted to press charges, but Dad insisted that she was asking for it.

Luckily, Mom kept plenty of pills in the medicine cabinet. She wasn't sure what all the prescriptions were for—and Mom had probably lost track herself, there were so *many* of them—so each bottle got upended onto the coffee table.

The last thing she saw as the room got all fuzzy after downing all the pills was Dad—

Except Dad didn't look like Dad, he was too young. And Dad was bald, so why'd he have a full head of hair? And his eyes were the wrong color . . .

Sam . . .

. . . he couldn't believe it. A *doll*. Of all the places to entrap him, they chose a *doll*.

It was just ridiculous papal propaganda. They kept calling what he did "satanic," but Satan had nothing to do with it. After all, God created all things, did He not? If so, that meant that the spells that he cast were also from God, not from Lucifer.

But the priests and the cardinals insisted, and he was condemned. Never mind what he had learned about Monsignor Theodore. He was just a heretic and a worshipper of the black arts, no one would believe *him* when he said that the monsignor had children by four different young women of the parish. Did no one notice how many women gave birth to red-haired children, despite their husbands' being off fighting Prime Minister Aberdeen's war in the Crimean Peninsula?

No, instead he was condemned to be burned at the stake. Knowing he'd be denied heaven, he had been surprised to find his spirit descending, not into hell, but into a doll made by a Bahamian housekeeper of the monsignor's. *It seems I wasn't the only one practicing the dark arts.*

Trapped in the *thing* of cloth and straw, he went to the Bahamas, then to the Americas, eventually finding himself in the thrall of a small child. By then it had been several decades, and he was going mad.

After the boy grew up and eventually went mad himself and died—and he was very proud of the rôle he played in the former—he was left inside the little room that the boy had had made for him. People would come and gape and point and be amused at the little room with the little furniture.

Today, one group of people walked in, led by a tall young man with hazel eyes and a mop of hair.

"And this is Raymond."
Sam . . .

. . . he lay awake in his bedroom in the White House, staring at the ceiling. The rhythm of his wife Bess sleeping beside him was all he could hear.

This was the only time he ever allowed himself to have doubts, here in the privacy of his bedroom, with only a sleeping Bess for company.

Did I do the right thing?

When the reporters asked him about bombing Hiroshima, he was adamant that it was the correct order to give. Back when he was an artillery officer, they used to call the Great War "the war to end all wars," and this latest conflict had proven that to be dead wrong. It had dragged on for years now, and it had to end. The Germans had surrendered in May, and it was long past time that the Japanese—who had brought the U.S. *into* this war in the first place by bombing American soil—did likewise. Their boys—*his* boys—were dying, and it needed to stop.

His mantra had always been "don't ever apologize for anything," and he never *would* apologize for what he had ordered. Not to the people of Japan, who had bombed Pearl Harbor, and not to the American people, who were made safer by his actions.

But here, now, alone in the dark, he wondered if what he had done was the right thing.

Stop being an ass, he admonished himself. *You're the commander in chief. The buck stops here, and you did right.*

Quietly, he climbed out of bed and walked to the door. He'd get one of the men outside to bring him a glass of warm milk, and he'd get some shut-eye.

Opening the door, he saw a very tall young man with far too much hair and hazel eyes. "Can I help you, sir?" he asked politely.

Sam . . .

. . . he stood over Agnes's deathbed, wondering what he would do with himself now.

The whole point of everything had been so he could retire, sell the boat, and spend his waning years with Agnes in their beautiful house.

However, the consumption didn't seem to care about his plans.

It had all happened so *fast*. One moment Agnes was in the sitting room, writing a letter to their son, while he sat on the front porch reading the newspaper and watching the carriages go by the cobblestone road in front of the house. Then she said she felt poorly and went upstairs to the bedroom to lie down. But she could not get to sleep for all the coughing.

When she started to cough up blood, he had summoned a physician.

Unfortunately, all the doctor could do was tell him what he suspected from the moment she started coughing blood: She had the consumption, and there was nothing to be done.

Now she lay dead in their bedroom, and he was alone. The house had been the perfect size when he had it built with his earnings on the wrecker, perfect for raising a family. Even when the children had grown up and moved away to start their own families, the house was always filled with just the two of them, plus whatever friends or family might visit.

Now, though, the house was empty.

He didn't know what to do.

"Excuse me, Captain?" said the voice of the man from the mortuary.

Turning around, he saw a tall young man with dark hair and hazel eyes. "Yes?"

"We're ready to take your wife."

Sam . . .

. . . he stood watching the munitions factory burn, the acrid smell burning his nostrils. He ran toward the building, looking for survivors to take back to his ambulance. He'd only just arrived in Milan, having volunteered to serve as an ambulance driver for the Red Cross.

Paris had been bad enough, with Jerry's shells blasting all around them as he and his friends tried to sightsee, but then *this* . . .

He ran toward the fire, finding only the dead. When he saw the corpse of a girl, it brought him up short.

War was men's work. There shouldn't have been girls here. Young men died in war, he knew that. Only eighteen years of age, he had volunteered as an ambulance driver—despite the fool at the Red Cross who insisted that he needed spectacles—in order to help both the living and the dead who fought in this Great War. Those who were wounded needed help, and those who died deserved proper burials, not having their corpses left on a battle-field.

Getting to his knees, he got the girl's body away from the fire. She was dead, but that was no reason to desecrate her further.

He was directed to an improvised mortuary that had been hastily assembled near the burned-out remains of the factory. No matter how many bodies he and the others brought back, it always seemed there were more, men and girls alike.

Then he ran back and found a familiar-looking young man in a soldier's uniform. He had unusually shaggy brown hair under his helmet and hazel eyes that stared blankly at the smoky sky.

Sam . . .

* * *

. . . he loved flirting with the tourists of both sexes when they came into the shop. Even after he was diagnosed with HIV, and even after he started losing weight and the crap broke out on his skin, he stayed on the job, selling silly T-shirts and sillier souvenirs to the tourists on Duval Street. Marty said he could keep working as long as he could stand upright. Based on the way he'd been coughing his lungs out, it wouldn't be for much longer.

But he was determined to make the most of it.

One tall drink of water came sauntering in, with shaggy brown hair and just to *die* for hazel eyes, and he came right up to him. "Can I help you?"

"I'm looking for a T-shirt for my brother."

Sam . . .

. . . he only felt alive when he was writing. Sitting at the kitchen table in the tiny cottage he rented, the fountain pen his aunt had given him in his hand, the notebook in front of him, and the verses just *flowing*.

He'd only gotten a few of his poems published, and it hardly paid the bills, but he didn't care, as long as he could write. All day, he would do his work as a janitor at the courthouse, but at night, he wrote his poems, and he was *alive*.

There was a knock at the door. "Hey, it's me. Got a package for ya."

He got up to open the door and saw the UPS guy. But he had shaggier hair, and was taller.

Sam . . .

. . . she loved the crowds more than anything. Sure, sometimes they didn't tip well, and sometimes they forgot to applaud, and sometimes they were downright rude, and sometimes they requested "Free Bird" for the eight millionth time, but overall, playing guitar in the Bull was just a great experience.

Tonight, though, was pretty dead. She plucked away at her Takamine acoustic that had gone with her to every gig. After finishing playing "Me and Julio Down By the Schoolyard" for the couple at the front table, she noticed that somebody else had come in, sitting at the bar: a tall guy, hunched over a lite beer.

She asked, "Any requests?"

"You know 'Brown-Eyed Girl,' lady?"

Sam . . .

They kept coming *at* him. Dean thought he would lose himself in the dead.

Mel Fisher, the famous treasure-seeker. Althea McNamara, a teenager who committed suicide after being gang-raped. Raymond, the doll who'd attacked them at Cayo Hueso, who turned out to be possessed by a nineteenth-century sorcerer named Caleb Dashwood. President Harry S Truman, after he dropped the A-bomb on Japan. Ernest Hemingway, when he volunteered for the Red Cross in World War I. José Sandoval, a gay store worker who died of AIDS. Jonathan Gomez, a poet. Bonnie Bowers, a Duval Street musician who died in a diving accident.

And so many more . . .

But Dean focused on Sam. No matter what, he had to save Sam, and that enabled Dean to get the dead under control.

When he did so, Dean felt it.

It was a rush like nothing he'd ever experienced. Better than the highest high, a bigger thrill than anything Dean could imagine. The entire world was at his fingertips. Even though the spirits were remnants of the dead, what Dean took from them was their joys, their hopes, their dreams, their doubts, their confusion, their grief, their anguish, their love, their hate, their *lives*.

All of it coursing through Dean.

He thought he'd felt alive before, but he was oh-so-wrong. While their lives were pretty miserable much of the time, Dean still got a rush from the hunt, from the destruction of evil, from the saving of lives. But that rush suddenly paled in comparison. It was like he had been color-blind his whole life, and suddenly could see every hue in a prism. He didn't just see the street, the construction site, the sky, the ocean—he saw *everything*. The electric currents running through power lines. Radio waves moving through the air. Ley lines coursing through the earth.

The first thing he did was project this new power onto the wards the Last Calusa had put up, shattering them with a flash of light.

Unsurprisingly, that got the Last Calusa's attention. The spirit appeared before Dean.

"Hey, Tonto," Dean said with a wicked grin. "You impressed yet?"

NINETEEN

The Last Calusa remembered.

For many seasons, the Calusa were the mightiest warriors. The Last Calusa remembered that because it was the reason for their vengeance. It was their reason for being.

The outsiders came, and the Calusa rejected them. The worst were their priests—"missionaries," they called themselves—who tried to turn them to the way of their one god. They even went so far as to insist that the eye soul of their god's only son and another eye soul of indeterminate origin were, along with their god, simply a different face of the Three Gods.

But the Calusa rejected their god. The Calusa thanked the Three Gods for what they granted. The outsiders simply begged their god for forgiveness for their transgressions. Worse, their god *granted* it, giving them free rein to commit more transgressions, secure in the knowledge that their weak and feeble god would still accept them if they bent their knee to him.

Worse, the outsiders knew nothing of the spirit world. Oh, they claimed to believe in two different afterworlds of the dead, one for those who transgressed, one for those who did not, and they all hoped to get into the latter so their eye souls would not suffer.

When the Last Calusa began their task, they learned that the outsiders had won the day, and taken over the land that once was the exclusive purview of the Calusa. They knew even less of the spirit world than they had before.

The dark spirits tried to control the Last Calusa, to turn them to their foul ways, but the Last Calusa's vengeance was too strong. One dark spirit was dead, killed by its own power turned back on it.

Now the sun was about to disappear, and the Last Calusa would be able to wreak their vengeance. The outsiders would pay for what they did.

Suddenly, the wards were shattered. The Last Calusa were briefly stunned by this, as none in this world of ignorance could possibly have the power to do that, and the dark spirit that the Last Calusa had not killed was too weakened by their own attack on it.

When the Last Calusa went to the source of the attack, they saw the dead soul. Brother to one of the sacrifices, the Last Calusa saw that he was tainted by the dark spirits, who had already claimed his life for their own. The Last Calusa could not sacrifice him, so they left him.

Now, though, the dead soul had changed. The eye souls of many flowed within him, and they all had the stink of the dark spirit.

The Last Calusa's belief that none knew of the spirit world in this time and place was apparently a false one.

But vengeance needed to be satisfied. The many dead cried out for it, and their song sang through the Last Calusa.

They sang that song to the Three Gods, and they began the dance.

Dean saw what the Last Calusa was doing, and said, "Nuh-uh, Tonto. No rain dance for you."

Combat instincts that came, not just from Dean and a lifetime of training by John Winchester, ex-Marine, but also from the spirits of dozens of naval officers, not to mention former artillery officer Harry S Truman, all became focused into a single blast of spiritual energy, and Dean took it and threw it at the Last Calusa.

It had no effect.

"Screw this," Dean said, and did it again.

Still, the Last Calusa continued their dance and their chant, unaffected.

Jonathan Gomez's spirit whispered into Dean's ear. *Violence without passion doesn't mean nothin'. It's just anger that's all over the place.*

Heeding the poet's advice, Dean brought forth Mel Fisher's passion for treasure seeking, Bonnie's passion for playing music, Jonathan's passion for his poetry, Hemingway's passion for the many loves of his life, and more.

Again, he struck the Last Calusa.

Though they continued the dance, the Last Calusa did stumble, both physically and verbally.

Lightning crackled across the twilight sky, and clouds came rolling in seemingly from nowhere.

Christ, it really was *a rain dance.*

Raising their arms to the darkening sky, the Last Calusa bellowed, "It begins!"

"Like hell." The protective instincts of Truman, who wanted to keep his people safe, of Hemingway, who wanted to safeguard the lives of soldiers when he drove the ambulance, of Captain Naylor, who always put the crews of his wreckers before himself, and of Dean his own self toward Sam came to the fore, and Dean was able to create wards of his own around Sam and the others under the tarp.

Thunder boomed, echoing off the sea, even as the lightning struck Dean's wards—but did not penetrate them.

Turning to face Dean through their freaky mask,

the Last Calusa said, "You will not deny us our vengeance!"

"Watch me." The passion, the combativeness, the protectiveness, Dean wrapped it up all into a ball and thrust it at the Last Calusa, who stumbled backward away from the construction site. Dean moved forward, the spirits flowing through him, and he kept at it. Truman's surety that dropping one atom bomb would not be enough, the soldier's instinct to make sure that the enemy was well and truly defeated, Dean's own knowledge that you had to make sure the creature of the night you fought was all dead, not just mostly dead, all combined to make him hammer away at the Last Calusa.

The lightning and thunder crashed down all around them, and a hard rain started to pelt South Street. Dean couldn't feel it touch his person, but he could sense the power of the storm, see it strike the pavement and the dirt with more intensity than even a typical Florida rainstorm generally managed. So sudden was the onslaught of the rain that Dean hesitated for only the briefest of seconds.

Then came the pain.

Dean had suffered plenty of pain in his life. He'd been beaten up, beat down, shot at, stabbed, cut, electrocuted, punched, kicked, bit, thrown across more rooms than he could count, and run over by a Mack truck.

If you combined all that pain, it was only a frac-

tion of what Dean felt now. The flip side of feeling
everything like this was that—well, he *really* did
feel everything. Perception was magnified, and so
was agony.

No matter how bad it got, though, he refused to
let the protection for Sam and the others falter. It
didn't matter if he died in the effort—he was dead
anyhow—but that sonofabitch wasn't taking Sam
with him.

And then the pain grew worse, in tandem with
the intensity of the rain. It was coming down hard
enough to dent the roofs of the police cruisers (but
not, Dean dimly but proudly noted, the Impala's).

Despair started to overwhelm him, and that,
too, was made worse by the spirits of the dead.
Hemingway's manic depressiveness that led to his
suicide, Althea's devastation at being gang-raped
and no one believing her that led to *her* suicide, the
degeneration of José as AIDS ravaged his body, the
terror of Caleb when the church condemned him to
death, all combined with Dean's own usually hidden
despair over his inevitable trip to hell to crush him.

He almost gave in.

Sam . . .

Dean shoved the despair into the back of his
mind where he kept his own fears and doubts,
and instead tapped into Bonnie's music, Jonathan's
poetry, Mel's obsession, Hemingway's lust for life,
and fought back.

It wasn't enough.

Crap. Where'd he get this power from?

And only then did Dean realize that the Last Calusa had that power all along—he just hadn't cut loose on Dean at first.

But Dean refused to give up. He drew upon the stubbornness of Truman, who spent most of his political career not being taken seriously, of Hemingway, whose obstinacy cost him more than one marriage, of Bonnie, who dealt with all the tribulations of being a woman in a male-dominated art, of José, who kept his chirpy optimism throughout most of his dying days, of Jonathan, who never gave up the dream of being a famous poet even though he died a janitor, of Caleb, who never let go of his anger and frustration. And he drew on his own stubbornness, which could be a wonder to behold.

All of that, he fed into keeping Sam safe. That was what was important.

Then the pain increased *again,* and Dean screamed to the heavens, the rain pelting into his open mouth . . .

Bobby Singer had seen a lot in his life, but nothing quite like this before. All of his hairs—on his head under his ball cap, his beard, the back of his neck—were standing on end.

He stood on the sidewalk facing the tableau,

across the street from the construction site, parallel to where the demon was hovering over the pentagram. To the right, Dean was fighting the Last Calusa.

All three were glowing. A line of spiritual energy no thicker than a fishing line connected the demon to Dean. It had gotten dark in a hurry thanks to the rainstorm the Last Calusa called down on them, and all the nearby streetlights were out, but South Street was lit up like a Christmas tree. The glow around Kat was a fire orange color, as was the link between her and Dean. Dean himself was more red. In both cases, the flame-related color probably had something to do with the origins of the demon's power.

The glow around the Last Calusa was blue. Bobby had no idea what *that* meant . . .

Two things had Bobby worried.

The first was that Dean appeared to be losing. He'd gained the upper hand for about half a second, but the Last Calusa came from behind in a hurry.

Dean's scream was as soul-chilling a sound as Bobby had ever heard. And that was against some mighty stiff competition. Worse, the glow around him dimmed to a fainter, lighter red, while the Last Calusa's became a cobalt blue.

However, the second thing was the bigger concern. Bobby had seen Dean come back from farther down in a fight, and he was willing to hang on to a hope that he might still triumph.

But then he took another gander at Kat, who was not looking at all well. Blood was trickling out of her nose and eyes and mouth. Her silky brown hair was getting stiff and strawlike. Blisters started to break out on her arms and stomach and legs.

The demon was burning out her host. And while she could always get a new one—Bobby himself was charmed against it, but he wouldn't be surprised if the demon had kept a human nearby in reserve—the break the demon would have to take to leave Kat and enter the new host would likely be fatal to Dean.

And there was always the possibility that Bobby's charm wouldn't work, and the demon *would* possess him.

The notion chilled Bobby something fierce. There wasn't much that scared Bobby anymore, but that was on the short list. He would rather die than go the way of his wife, of Sam, of Meg . . .

Bobby kept the Colt ready. And kept himself ready for whatever might come.

Sam broke completely free right before he heard his brother scream.

He'd heard Dean's taunting arrival on the scene, and from the sounds of it, he had some kind of mystical mojo on his side. *Oh God, did he actually take up Fedra on her offer?* Urged on by this thought, and by his success in moving one hand, Sam pushed hard against the Last Calusa's force, and eventually fell face-first onto the ground. He'd been still for so long that the rough taste of dirt was actually pleasant.

The cops and lab techs were still immobilized. "What'd you do?" "How'd you do that?" "Christ, get *us* outta here, willya?"

Sam clambered to his feet and moved as if to run toward the tarp, but just as quickly as he'd freed himself he was trapped again. He was stuck in midrun, and his body started to slowly move back into position in the circle with the others.

"Oh no you don't," Sam said through gritted teeth as he fought against the Last Calusa, trying to will his long legs not to move, to stand still, to do what *he* wanted.

Blinding pain ripped through his skull, much like the headaches he used to get with his visions, as he tried to fight against the Last Calusa. Somewhere during this, it had started raining, hard, and the staccato rhythm of the rain slapping against the tarp echoed in Sam's ears in time with the pounding in his head.

Then he heard Dean scream.

"Dean!" Sam cried, even though he doubted that his brother could hear him. But he used the anguish of his cry to egg himself onward, to push against the Last Calusa.

And then he fell forward once again, as did all the others.

"God, I can *move*!" "How the hell—?" "Ow, my leg!" "How'd that happen?"

Sam immediately ran out to the tarp, pushed it aside, felt the rain pelt down on him—

—and saw his brother *glowing* while screaming. And then light shot out of his fingers and hit the Last Calusa.

Every time I think I've seen everything, something comes along and raises the damn bar, Sam thought, staring at the agonized face of his brother. He also saw Bobby across the street pointing the Colt at a woman who was hovering over the pavement. The woman had the black eyes that signaled demonic possession, and was above a reverse pentagram. Sam also noted that there seemed to be a glowing string connecting the woman to Dean.

He really did do the deal with Fedra. Desperate times, I guess . . .

In that moment, Sam realized that he'd been an idiot.

For two years, Sam had been displaying psychic powers that linked him to Azazel, and also to other children who, like Sam, had been touched by the demon. Sam had been concerned that entire time that he was somehow unclean, different— evil. Dean kept insisting—as he did fairly often, truth be told—that Sam was being a jackass.

Now, he saw Dean, almost literally charged up by a spell being cast by a demon. Sam could *feel* the power that Dean was now channeling—so could the Last Calusa, to his detriment, though the Native spirit was giving as good as he got.

Despite this, there was no doubt in Sam's mind that his brother was in there and that he was—well, not all right, but still Dean. Just as Dean saw that, premonitions or not, he was still Sam.

But Dean couldn't do this alone. Luckily, he no longer had to. Dean's attacks had obviously either weakened the Last Calusa, or simply forced the spirit to draw on the energy needed to hold the sacrifices in place in order to defeat Dean. So Sam was free to do his part.

He made a beeline for the Impala, which was parked right on the street. He considered checking the cop cars, which were closer, but this was Florida—they wouldn't have what he'd need.

Bobby noticed Sam running toward the car, and called out, "Sam?"

Running to the trunk, Sam dug his set of keys out of his pocket and opened the Impala's trunk, rainwater sluicing down the sides of the car as the trunk was lifted. Digging around, he found the bag of salt they kept back there for just such an occasion, as well as a can of lighter fluid.

"Sam, what the hell're you doin'?" Bobby asked, as Sam ran back to the construction site.

"Whatever I can," Sam said.

Once back under the tarp, Sam, clothes and hair now sopping wet, ran straight for the unearthed bones.

"What the heck're you doin'?" one cop asked.

Ignoring him, Sam ripped open the bag of salt and upended it onto the Calusa bones. Once the bag was empty, and every exposed bone was covered in salt, Sam unscrewed the lighter-fluid can.

"You're salting and burning the bones, aren't you?" another cop asked.

A lab tech said, "Hang on, you said that wouldn't kill it."

"It won't," Sam said after he'd sprayed the fluid around enough of the bones. Then he pulled a matchbook out of his pocket, yanked one free, lit it, and dropped it onto the bones, grateful that the tarp was keeping the rain out.

"Then why you bothering?"

Sam shoved his wet hair out of his eyes with one hand. "You know what they say—that which does not kill you still hurts a helluva lot."

The Last Calusa screamed as a part of them burned away.

They did not know how this had happened, but the pain was blinding. It was as if the Calusa were dying all over again, one by one being removed from the Last Calusa as they had been removed by the outsiders' diseases and guns.

Gathering up their strength, the Last Calusa patched the hole that this event had made, making themselves whole again.

But that took time, and it took effort, and doing so left them vulnerable to the dead soul.

Out of the corner of his mind, Dean had seen Sam running to the Impala and returning with salt and lighter fluid. *That's my brother,* Dean thought, proud that Sam had broken free, prouder still that he was pitching in. While it was true that salting and burning the bones wouldn't kill the Last Calusa, it'd probably still have an effect. The spirit of Caleb whispered to Dean, *Yes, that will weaken this foul creature. Perhaps then we can gain the upper hand.*

Sure enough, Dean heard the roar of the flames as the lighter-fluid-soaked salted skeletons alighted, and felt the Last Calusa diminish. For that matter, he saw it: Once Sammy started the bone barbecue, the Last Calusa was back to the height he'd been at when he'd come into the Fedregottis' hotel room.

Given the opening, Dean pulled it all together: the passion and the pain, the stubbornness and the optimism, the pugilism and the pacifism, the despair and the hope, and gathered it into a single blow.

"Okay, Tonto, this is it. Just one of us is gonna walk outta here alive, and it sure as hell ain't gonna be you!"

For the American people . . .
For my poor Agnes . . .
For all the boys who didn't make it . . .
For Mom and Dad . . .
For all those tourists I flirted with . . .
For the music . . .
For the thrill of the chase . . .
For Sam . . .
Dean poured it all into one shot.

Bobby watched the tableau through the rain that poured from the sky and dripped from the bill of his ball cap. The Last Calusa's blue glow dimmed, and the spirit itself got smaller shortly after Sam ran back into the construction site. *Good work there, kiddo*, he thought, even as Dean's glow intensified into a blood red, and he hit the Last Calusa with seemingly everything he had."

Dean's scream before had been primal and bone-chilling. But the Last Calusa's scream in response to Dean's attack made the earlier one seem like a mild whimper. Bobby felt it in his gut.

The glow around the Last Calusa dimmed to almost nothing, and the spirit's flesh became translucent.

Bobby stole a glance at the demon, who was smiling with a feral glee. Her hair was lustrous again, the bleeding had stopped, and the blisters were gone.

Dean's face had constricted into a rictus of pain and determination, and he started yelling—but not in pain. It was the cry of adrenaline, like when martial artists shouted before they broke blocks of ice with their hands.

Then came a massive flash of light, and Bobby was blinded. He clamped his eyes shut and held his arm over his face, but even through his lids and arm he could see the light.

He hoped it was the discharge of the Last Calusa discorporating.

When the light dimmed, Bobby blinked several dozen times to banish the spots of the afterglow.

The rain had stopped.

Sam poked his head through the tarp. Behind him, Bobby could see the flames licking upward.

The demon was now standing on the pavement, still smiling. Of the pentagram, there was no sign, only burned and broken pavement.

Dean just stood there, staring off into space.

Moving toward him, Bobby said, "Dean, you okay?" even as Sam ran out, and said, "Dean!"

"Ah ah *ah*!" the demon said, and suddenly Bobby was flying backward onto the South Street sidewalk.

Getting quickly to his feet, Bobby saw that Sam had been similarly knocked down.

"Sorry, boys," the demon said, "but playing-well-with-others time is *over*. The Last Calusa's power is mine, and so is my not-so-willing vessel. Isn't that right, Dean?"

Dean kept staring straight ahead. "Screw you, bitch." But Bobby could tell it was a struggle.

Hell with this, Bobby thought as he aimed the Colt and fired it at the demon, silently praying to Kat for forgiveness.

The bullet flew through the air and then stopped. A second later, it fell to the pavement with a clink, its momentum gone.

"Nice try, Bobby-baby, but you can't kill what you can't touch. C'mon, Dean. We need to get some supplies from your hotel room, then we're off to the races."

Dean turned and, robotlike, walked toward the Impala.

Sam screamed, "Dean!" and ran toward his brother, only once again to be thrown aside by demonic power.

At the demon's command, Dean got behind the wheel of the Impala, while Kat got into the passenger side. Within moments, the car had turned around and was streaking down South Street toward Duval. Bobby and Sam had both tried to run toward it, but couldn't get within ten feet of the vehicle.

"Son of a *bitch*!" Thanks to the charm Bobby had given to the Winchesters—which they had since gotten tattooed on their chests—neither Dean nor Sam could be possessed by a demon, but a demon as powerful as this one could easily take control of Dean's body.

And they'd just gotten away with their only car.

"C'mon," Sam said, starting to run after the car, "it's only a mile to the B&B."

Bobby chased after Sam, if only because that was the only way to keep talking to him. "Sam, there's no point! By the time we get there on foot, they'll be gone!"

But Sam kept running.

With an annoyed grunt, Bobby ran after him.

TWENTY

Sam was fairly winded by the time they made it to Eaton Street. He and Bobby had been running up Duval, land-sharking their way around tourists and barhoppers, none of whom were particularly inclined to get out of the way of two people who had the bad taste to be *running* down a party street.

Somewhere along the line, Bobby had twigged to why there was a chance of finding Dean and the demon still present at the Naylor House. "But," Bobby said between deep breaths, "we gotta assume the worst."

If the worst happened, Sam would deal with it then, but he was fairly certain that "Fedra" was too arrogant to notice.

When they got to the Naylor House, Sam was relieved to see that the Impala was still parked in front of the B&B. Nicki and Bodge were in the front room, reading. At their entrance, Snoopy, who had been lying on the floor, bounded to his feet and ran over to Sam and Bobby, hoping to be scratched.

"Uh, Samwise, you may wanna be careful," Bodge said with a big grin. "Dean-ola brought a fine dish home, and I think they want some alone time."

Not wanting to get into it with her, Sam just made a noncommittal grunt, extricated himself from the enthusiastic sheepdog, and dashed to the garden entrance in the back, Bobby on his heels.

Sam was even more relieved when he didn't see anyone standing outside the bungalow where the brothers' rooms were. He jumped up onto the porch and slid the door open, but didn't enter.

Dean was still standing ramrod-straight, though he now had a smile on his face. "Good to see you, Sammy."

"Likewise," Sam said.

Kat ran for the door, but stopped short—right under the circumference of the Key of Solomon that Dean and Sam had inscribed on the ceiling when they got back from the Hyatt.

Bobby had been the first to tell them of the Key. It was a Devil's Trap, an elaborate circle that would keep any demon inside it. Usually, it was used by hunters as a trap to keep the demon still while an exorcism was performed.

Which was Sam's plan right now.

Knowing this, Kat screamed, "Don't you *dare* do this! I will *kill* your brother! If you don't break the seal on the trap, I will snap his neck like a dry twig!"

Sam said the only thing he could in response. "*Regna terrae, cantate Deo, psallite Domino qui fertis super caelum caeli ad Orientem Ecce dabit voci Suae vocem virtutis, tribuite virtutem Deo.*"

"If you coulda killed him, you woulda," Bobby said. "My guess? You can't."

"You really think I won't kill this little mutt?"

Once, Sam would have needed Dad's notebook, but he'd done enough of these that he could probably exorcise a demon in his sleep at this point. "*Exorcizamus te, omnis immundus spiritus omnis satanica potestas, omnis incursio infernalis adversarii, omnis legio, omnis congregatio et secta diabolica. Ergo draco maledicte et omnis legio diabolica adjuramus te cessa decipere humanas creaturas, eisque aeternae Perditionis venenum propinare.*"

Smoke started to issue forth from Kat's eyes and mouth and ears. "No! It won't end like this! I won't *let* it!"

"Sorry, sister," Dean said. "It's not like you need me. Way I figure it, you snuff me without permission from whoever the crossroads demon was workin' for, you might get yourself in a bit of a bind."

"*Vade, Satana, inventor et magister omnis fallaciae, hostis humanae salutis. Humiliare sub potenti manu dei, contremisce et effuge, invocato a nobis sancto et terribili nomine, quem inferi tremunt. Ab insidiis diaboli, libera nos, Domine. Ut Ecclesiam tuam secura tibi facias libertate servire, te rogamus, audi nos. Ut inimicos sanctae Ecclesiae humiliare digneris, te rogamus, audi nos.*"

Kat stumbled to the floor, then got to her feet and slapped Dean, who was unable to recoil from the blow. "Nice try, kiddo, but after what I just went through? Being bitch-slapped ain't exactly something I'm gonna get all sore over."

"No! Noooooooooo!"

Sam smiled as he finished the exorcism. "*Ut inimicos sanctae Ecclesiae te rogamus, audi nos. Terribilis Deus de sanctuario suo. Deus Israhel ipse truderit virtutem et fortitudinem plebi Suae. Benedictus Deus. Gloria Patri.*"

At "*Patri,*" Kat's head reared back and black smoke poured out of her mouth toward the ceiling, only to disappear into the Key of Solomon.

Then the girl crumpled to the floor, unconscious.

Dean, now able to move, knelt and checked her pulse. "She's alive, but we should probably get her to a hospital."

"I'll do it," Bobby said. "I ain't wanted by nobody, so I'll—"

"Actually," Dean said, "just tell Nicki and Bodge up front. They'll take care of it."

Sam felt a bit odd about that. "You sure?"

"Trust me, Sammy, we can count on those two."

Bobby moved back toward the house. "I'll take care of it."

"Okay." Sam hesitated, then stared at his older brother. "Are *you* all right?"

"I'll be honest with you, Sammy—that was *seriously* trippy. I don't remember all of it—it's a blur of weird memories and crazy emotions and . . ." Dean shuddered. "I dunno." He got to his feet. "Hey, thanks for the bone-burning."

Shrugging, Sam said, "Somebody had to save your ass." Stifling a yawn, Sam added, "I don't know about you, Dean, but I'm ready to nap for a year."

"Not me. I'm wired like you wouldn't believe."

"You looked it." Sam stared at Dean and noticed that his hair was all spiky and standing on end. "Still do, really."

Dean frowned, then looked at himself in the mirror. "Jesus." He started trying to mat down his hair with his hands, but it kept springing back up.

Chuckling, Sam said, "C'mon, you look hip."

"Yeah, if this was 1985 London. Crap." Dean took a breath. "Well, I don't care. I just kept the spirit of a long-dead Indian tribe from wiping out most of humanity, and that calls for a beer. Or six. You comin'?"

Sam held up his hands. Given the mood Dean was in, Sam suspected that he would only crimp his older brother's style. "I'll pass. You go ahead, I'll wait here for the ambulance to take Kat."

"Yeah." Dean looked down at her. "She should be okay."

"Maybe. Depends on how much she remembers. I mean, *we're* used to this."

"Not this," Dean said. "This was—different. It was like I had hundreds of people in my head." He shuddered. "And you know what? Hemingway really *was* an asshole."

When Dean woke up, it was like a freight train was running in circles in his brain.

The sun was blaring through the window of the Naylor House bungalow, blinding him and causing a sharp pain right behind his left eye. His mouth felt like he'd been chewing cotton.

He moved to sit up, and only then did he register that he wasn't in bed alone.

After staring at the naked female body for a few seconds, light finally dawned. "Oh yeah."

He'd gone back to Captain Tony's. Grande Skim Latte was playing there again, and this time Dean met a woman named Bess.

No, stupid, her name is Martha. Shaking his head, he thought, *Agnes? Marty? Gene? Sue?*

All of those were people that were loved by the spirits who'd filled his mind during the fight against the Last Calusa. The memories were fading, but those names stayed prominent—not surprising, really, since the feelings associated with them were really intense.

Whoever this woman was, though, she looked *damn* hot while sleeping. She slept on her side, accentuating the curve of her hips, her arms hugging the pillow to her head. Bits of memories of the night before flashed in Dean's mind's eye: slow-dancing with her during a rendition of Clapton's "Wonderful Tonight," daring her to donate her bra to the wall and watching her take it off while not removing her shirt, doing shots of—well, something, then stumbling back to the Naylor House for a considerable amount of sex.

A gentle tapping at the door echoed in Dean's entire skull, and he peered at the door to see Sammy. Grasping about for his underpants, Dean climbed into them and went to the door, shutting it behind him. Putting a finger to his lips, he whispered, "She's asleep."

Sam looked like he was about to say something, then thought better of it. "Just got off the phone with Bobby at the hospital. He said Kat'll be all right. She says she doesn't remember what happened."

"That'd be a nice change." Dean knew that most of those possessed remembered it all. That was part of the torment, after all. But this girl may have just repressed it.

"And I talked to Officer Montrose, and he and his coworkers are writing up last night as a freak rainstorm. The deaths are gonna stay open cases to keep the politicians happy, but they know that it won't ever be solved."

"Cool. So our work here is done?"

"Not quite," said a voice from behind him.

Whirling around, Dean saw the spirit of Captain Naylor. "Captain!" Then Dean frowned. "You're still coherent."

"Which is more than I can say for you, Mr. Winchester," Naylor said with a smile. "I assume your distasteful fornications are complete, and you can get on with the business of fulfilling your end of our bargain?"

"Uh, yeah, sure." Dean blinked a few times. "Look, I need a shower, and to say *sayonara* to my friend here. Say we meet at the walnut tree where you're buried in an hour?"

"That is acceptable," Naylor said.

An hour later, Dean had wished the girl goodbye— he never did get her name, and couldn't think of a good way to ask, though he noticed that she never said *his* name, either—and showered. Meanwhile,

Sam went to Nicki and Bodge and explained why they needed to dig up the area around the walnut tree.

By the time Dean was out of the shower—and his hair was back to normal, thank *God*—and dressed, Bobby had returned from the hospital, and the three of them started digging around the tree in question. Eventually, they came across the remains.

"No coffin?" Sam said.

"It was my wish," Naylor said from behind them. "I wanted my remains to fertilize the house's garden."

Bodge, who had brought over a pitcher of ice water, said, "Well, they did a good job. It's a beautiful garden, Captain."

Nicki was present also, and added, "I'm sorry you won't consider staying. Having a ghost'd increase our bookings like you wouldn't believe!"

Dean knelt and, using a garden spade, cleared away the dirt from around Naylor's bones.

"That is quite distressing," Naylor said. Dean had to admit to finding Naylor's discomfort to be hilarious.

Sam spread salt on the bones while Bobby took care of the lighter fluid. Dean stood with his lighter, just about ready to get the roast started, when he hesitated. He wasn't used to doing this while the spirit was standing over him and approving of the whole procedure.

"Uh, anyone wanna say anything?" he asked lamely.

"As a matter of fact, Mr. Winchester, I would," Naylor said. "One doesn't often get the chance to speak at one's own funeral."

Putting the lighter back in his pocket, Dean said, "Go ahead, then."

"I do not know if I am bound for Paradise or elsewhere. It seems I have already spent time in purgatory, for I have been trapped in this place that I built for so long. But now, thanks to the graces of these good people, I may at last move on to my just reward. Regardless of where my soul is destined, I can say with assuredness that my life—my *after*-life, that is—has been enriched by these two young men, who have sacrificed so much. I'm proud to have known you both, Misters Winchester, and I hope you continue to be a beacon of hope in a dark world."

Dean hadn't expected quite so sentimental an outpouring from the old crank. But then, Dean had gotten a certain amount of insight into the captain as well, though it was fading now, and he said, "I don't think there's any doubt where you're going, Cap'n. It's been a privilege."

Naylor simply nodded.

After looking around at everyone else, Dean pulled out the lighter, flicked it alight, and bent over to ignite the bones.

Within a few seconds, the skeleton was burning, flames leaping toward the sky.

Captain Naylor faded from view.

"Rest in peace, Cap'n," Dean said.

They considered spending more time on the island, but Sam reminded Dean that there was a series of odd disappearances that happened in Neah Bay, Washington, every tenth of January. If they started immediately, they'd just make it to the Washington coast town—which was as far from Key West as it was possible to be and remain within the continental U.S.—in time.

After saying their good-byes to Nicki, Bodge, and Snoopy—the latter with many licks of Dean's face—and to Yaphet—who gave all three of them a free poem—Dean and Sam drove Bobby to the Key West Airport to catch his flight back to Sioux Falls.

"Good work, boys," Bobby said, giving each of the boys a hug. It was a little too emo for Dean, but for Bobby, he didn't mind so much.

Once Bobby went off to check in, Dean drove around the island to Route 1, and they headed northward through the Keys.

"You realize," Sam said as they started over the Seven-Mile Bridge, "that *all* the spirits are probably still supercharged? I mean, Naylor was still the way he was when we got there, even after we exorcised the demon."

"So Hemingway'll still be kicking cat lovers out of his house?" Dean asked with a grin.

"And Truman playing poker at the Little White House, and who knows *what* else? If nothing else, it'll probably keep Cayo Hueso Ghost Tours in business, even with the double homicide."

"Yeah." The breeze blew through Dean's hair as he reached into the pile of tapes trying to find the right one. "And thanks again for savin' my ass."

"Thanks for savin' mine," Sam said. "And I ain't gonna stop doing it, either."

"I know you won't." Dean sighed. "Hey, maybe the horse will talk."

"What?"

"Never mind." He finally found the tape he wanted and plunked it into the deck.

The strains of Van Morrison's "Brown-Eyed Girl" echoed through the Impala as they headed out of the Keys.

Author's Note

Those of you who bought my previous *Supernatural* novel, *Nevermore*, will recall that I provided a playlist that served as a soundtrack for reading the book. In the interests of laziness—and in getting those of you who *didn't* buy *Nevermore* to do so—I'm not going to reproduce that list here, but instead refer you to it as a starter for what to listen to while reading *Bone Key*. In addition, I would add the following tunes to that list:

The Animals: "House of the Rising Son"
Asia: "Heat of the Moment"
Bachman Turner Overdrive: "You Ain't Seen Nothin' Yet"
The Band: "Don't Do It" (either the version on *Rock of Ages* or *The Last Waltz*)

Boston: "Don't Look Back," "Foreplay/Long Time"

Creedence Clearwater Revival: "Run Through the Jungle"

The Charlie Daniels Band: "The Devil Went Down to Georgia"

The Doobie Brothers: "Long Train Runnin'"

Huey Lewis and the News: "Back in Time"

John Fogerty: "Eye of the Zombie"

Screamin' Jay Hawkins: "I Put a Spell on You"

Jethro Tull: "Pibroch (Cap in Hand)," "Some Day the Sun Won't Shine for You," "Valley"

Van Morrison: "Brown-Eyed Girl"

Queen: "Fat-Bottomed Girls," "One Vision"

Billy Squier: "The Stroke"

The Temptations: "Ball of Confusion (That's What the World is Today)"

Tom Waits: "Gun Street Girl," "Mr. Siegal," "Tango Till They're Sore"

There's an artist I first saw as the opening act for Mark Knopfler named Paul Thorn. You can check out his work at www.paulthorn.com, but every time I listen to his music, especially to his amazing album *Mission Temple Fireworks Stand*, I get a *Supernatural* vibe. So feel free to mix him in.

Finally, for Key West color, I recommend all the albums by Michael McCloud (www.michaelmccloud.com) and Black and Skabuddah (www.blackandskabuddah.com). The former plays practically every day at the Schooner's Wharf and is a Key West institution (he wrote "The Conch Republic Song" whence derives this book's epigraph). The latter, a pair of transplanted New Yorkers, used to play regularly at my favorite Key West saloon, Captain Tony's, and now are regulars at Sloppy Joe's. I've taken several trips to Key West over the years, and listening to my CDs by those two acts always serves as a pleasant reminder of that glorious island.

(And no, there's no Jimmy Buffett.)

—Keith R.A. DeCandido
Somewhere in New York City
January 2008